The Key to Tantalis

Michael Klerck

Order this book online at www.trafford.com
or email orders@trafford.com

Most Trafford titles are also available at major online book retailers.

Printed in the United States of America.

ISBN: 978-1-4269-3508-4 (sc)

ISBN: 978-1-4269-3509-1 (e-book)

*Our mission is to efficiently provide the world's finest, most comprehensive
book publishing service, enabling every author to experience success.
To find out how to publish your book, your way, and have it available
worldwide, visit us online at www.trafford.com*

Trafford rev. 6/24/2010

 www.trafford.com

North America & international
toll-free: 1 888 232 4444 (USA & Canada)
phone: 250 383 6864 ♦ fax: 812 355 4082

Acknowledgements:

The Flight of Dragons: I would like to acknowledge that the mechanism of dragon flight was first imagined by Peter Dickinson in his truly amazing book, The Flight of Dragons. I was so inspired by this publication that I became determined to include dragons in my writing.

The Power of Now: I would also like to acknowledge that the concept and the term Power of Now, was borrowed from Eckhart Tolle and his book of the same name. This book also inspired me to adopt what has become a lifelong challenge: to keep my focus on the present in order to allow its meaning and importance to overrule obsessions with the past or the future.

I should perhaps also acknowledge that the war-cry the evil Inkwish use is a loose adaptation of the same from my Alma Mater, South African College School (SACS, in Newlands Cape Town, 1972). No doubt had my old Latin master been alive today he might have taken some comfort in knowing that I have been able, at least, to look up the Latin quotations.

::: one :::
The Box

vulneratus, non victus
wounded, but not conquered

A wooden box. It had all started with one small, beautiful wooden box.

Few people might have paid much attention to it, except perhaps for the ornate carving on the front.

It was a box once buried, but now no longer under ground. It contained something of great value to many souls – a fact unknown to its owner, and it was a box that had been buried by someone who was no longer alive. A simple wooden box, however, that would change the current owner's life inextricably.

But more later.

Right now, Martin Fields was having a bad day. As his mother would say, he was not a happy camper. He had a project for tomorrow and his mother had his library cards in her wallet, and was late. What was worse, Martin had rammed his right hand against the frame of the kitchen door. It throbbed persistently and he was nursing it when his mother did finally arrive.

"Anyone home?"

Martin shook his head. The door was wide open and

Magnus, Martin's dog, was lying across the threshold – how could someone *not* be home he thought to himself.

"Mom, I'm here …" said Martin, with just a tiny edge to his voice.

"Oh, I'm so glad. I've got some great news to tell you …" She looked down. "What's wrong with your hand?" His mother paused just long enough to allow Martin to open his mouth to reply, but he didn't manage to get a word out before she continued. "Do you remember that odd-looking man Daddy used to have over for supper, to talk about money?"

Martin had his mind firmly on other things, and didn't want to encourage his Mother, so kept his mouth shut. He loved her more than anything in the world, but she could talk anyone round the bend and back, and now wasn't the time.

"Mom, I'm sorry to interrupt, but I really need to go."

"To the toilet, dear?"

"*No* … to the library. My project has to be in tomorrow," he said, with just a tiny edge of irritation in his voice.

"Oh yes, of course. I know, we'll go in a moment," said his mother, slowing down slightly while she unpacked a large yellow box of breakfast cereal into the white cupboard that served as a pantry. "Anyway, he telephoned me at work (his mother worked as a food technologist) and said that Daddy had started some trust thing … I never really did get to grips with money matters."

Mrs Fields stopped abruptly, looked down at Martin, still holding his elbow and shook her head.

"I'm sorry, Martin, I have gone on a bit, haven't I? Please don't tell me you jammed your hand in the doorway *again*."

Martin knew that there was no way of getting past this; he would simply have to indulge his mother until she had got off her chest whatever she wanted say. He took a deep breath, and smiled, which made his large brown eyes seem even smaller than usual.

"Yup; the doorframe; again."

His hand was feeling a little better although he continued to massage it. Mrs Field bent down and stroked it gently. Martin wanted to pull it away, but found her touch soothing.

"Anyway, about the money man and your father," she said.

Talk of his father always made him sad. It was not quite two years since the motor accident, and the death of his father. He sometimes felt guilty not wanting his mother to talk about him too much, realising only recently that it was her way of coming to terms with her own loss.

It had been something he had had to learn – that she had also lost someone dear to her.

"He used to come around and Daddy did some business with him, and to cut a long story short ...". Mrs Fields rose to her feet again, and continued unpacking more groceries. The packet of muffins didn't escape Martin's notice. "I have some wonderful news ...," She stopped again and looked down at Martin, "Daddy managed to provide for all your schooling and university one day. It's such a load off my shoulders." Mrs Fields was smiling broadly and feeling relieved at the thought.

"Mom, you really *are* strange, sometimes," said Martin, having regained his composure. "I love you very much, and am very glad Dad managed to save all that money. Of course, I knew he would, anyway; but I *must* get to the library before it closes."

Martin was already putting on his gloves.

"Wouldn't you rather I take you, dear?" asked his mother. Magnus had already decided on the proper course of action, and stood wagging his tail next to Martin's side. Take-me, take-me, take-me, his tail seemed to be saying, and just to make sure Martin understood he added a playful growl.

"I don't think so, Mom. By the time I get into the car and out the other end, I could make it there and back. Besides you don't like Magnus in the car." Martin bent over and ruffled Magnus's head, sending him into a dance of joyful anticipation. "Please give me my library card, and I'll be off."

The pavements were wide, smooth and without too many obstacles, such as traffic lights, or intersections, which meant that Martin, if he was concentrating, could make it from home to the library in less than three minutes. And best of all, Magnus only just managed to keep up with him. By now the neighbourhood could either hear or see Martin coming, and everyone got out of his way as quickly as possible. He was famous for his speed and agility and solicited waves from up, down and across every street.

It was the only fun part about being in a wheel-chair – he could give Magnus a good workout, and everyone made way for him!

Martin was smiling now; in his element. He lent forward and felt the muscles in his arms warming up, pumping slowly as he gripped each wheel and pushed downwards as hard as he could. It had taken practice; the first year had been terrible, but he had finally cracked it. His original wheel-chair had been slow and boring. And it had taken a lot to persuade the team at the hospital to give him a new one, built more for speed.

Luckily the library had a ramp. As Martin got to the top, Dominika emerged through the front door.   She opened her mouth to speak, but he stopped her.

"Hi! Sorry, can't stop now. Must do some stuff before the library closes! See you later," said Martin, pushing his chair over the threshold, and through the large wooden doors of the library.

He had made it. Suddenly the immense thick quietness overtook him and he had to sit for a while to rest and allow his breathing to slow down. His heart was still racing and he put his hand on his chest, as though to calm it. Magnus settled down; he knew exactly where he was and behaved like any well-trained dog should in a public library.

Martin loved it here. All the knowledge and mysteries of the world in once place – it was something like the internet, but even better. It had been the only place where he felt truly comfortable when he first ventured out into the world again after the accident.

Perhaps here he felt perfectly 'normal' because he could face everyone at eye level when they were seated. Perhaps it had been simply because Martin had always loved books, and reading; especially research. Looking up things, discovering pictures, drawings and paintings – knowledge and thoughts lost to the everyday world, and hiding quietly and secretly in this huge building.

His private castle.

Magnus, used to the quiet interior, positioned himself at Martin's side, stopping whenever he stopped to take a book. Martin had only another hour to complete the research he wanted to do on ancient Rome and its soldiers. He soon found the section

on ancient history. Now came the difficult part; even if he saw
what he wanted, he would have to ask someone to take the book
down off a shelf above him. He hated not being totally inde-
pendent.

With three books in his lap, he made for a table, and with
Magnus lying at his feet, he buried his head as deeply as he could.
It did not take him long to find what he was looking for. The project was based on a theme they had had all term: war; it was
pretty cool, because the Romans were some of the best warriors
in history, and invented many tactics used in modern warfare.
Martin's class had been able to choose any era, and any nation;
for Martin it had been a no-brainer – the Romans rocked! He had
finished most of the project itself, but wanted to add just a few
paragraphs on how their inventions had led to modern applica-
tions.

Martin knew he had more than he needed after just twenty
minutes, and as he was closing the largest of the three books in
front of him, something caught his eye.

It was a picture of – he was not quite sure, in fact – a large
bird-like creature; perhaps some ancient animal from Roman
times, thought Martin to himself. It looked a bit like a lizard.

No; a dinosaur. He could see that it had been drawn or
painted a long time ago – the kind of drawing sketched by an

unsophisticated hand. The picture of the creature was in a framed side-bar, to the right of the text.

And then, suddenly, Martin realised what it was. A dragon.

A little strange for a dragon, Martin thought; but definitely a dragon. Underneath, and in smaller text and in a different hand, he read the following words:
"The ancient Greeks and Romans believed that dragons had the ability to understand and to convey to mortals the secrets of the Earth."

Martin read the text, mouthing each word. "Secrets of the Earth?" What secrets could an animal teach the Romans, he wondered.

He continued to read: "partly as a result of this conception of the monster as a benign and powerful protective influence, and partly because of its fearsome qualities, it was employed as a military emblem. The Roman legions adopted it in the first century AD, inscribing the figure of a dragon on the standards carried into battle by the cohorts."

Martin stared at the picture for a long time. What was it that worried him? The texture of the creature looked typical of a dragon – lizard-like, with sharp protrusions running down its spine; they seemed to give it a balance, adding to its symmetry.

The wings; they were very small. Quite tiny, in fact.

Strange, thought Martin. Surely dragons should have large wings in order to fly – it looked huge? But then again he had nothing to compare it to – there was no person in the picture for reference. He was tempted to look for another book on dragons but decided against it when he noticed the time. Still he could not take his eyes off the picture.

Then he froze.

There was something else that suddenly caught his eye. He looked in astonishment at the foot of the tree in the picture, next to the dragon itself – there on the ground, right beneath the tree was a box. Not only was the tree itself familiar; similar to the old oak at the bottom of his own garden. But the box! Martin sat bolt upright, pushing himself away from the table suddenly.

No! surely not!

Magnus struggled to his feet. He peered up at his owner and friend, wondering what had happened.

Martin bent down and patted his head to reassure him, his hand shaking slightly. He took a deep breath to calm himself, then pulled himself forward towards the table, and looked at the picture again.

The box did not only look familiar – it seemed to be an exact replica of the one he and his father had buried when he was nine, just before the accident. At least this was true as far as

Martin could tell; it was, after all, quite small in the picture itself.

Made of wood, it had a metal frame that looked as if it was fashioned from gold, with ornamental carvings. One in particular – a set wings on the top – had an inscription below it: *Stultum est timere, quod vitare non potes.*

Martin said each word carefully to himself, from memory, as he had a hundred times, and then translated the Latin to himself – *it is foolish to fear what you cannot avoid.* Although Martin could not read or speak Latin fluently, his father had been able to, and he had often said something to Martin and then translated it. He had explained each word in the inscription, and they had often spent time pondering its meaning, and just how true it was. Perhaps it had been because his father had quoted the inscription repeatedly, or perhaps it was just because he had seen the box as a gift, but Martin had never forgotten the words themselves.

Especially in the last few months.

Of course, he could not see the inscription in the picture, it was too small, but the shape, the ornate metal frame and even what looked like the two carved wings were all reasonably clear. Martin shook his head, partly in disbelief, partly in fear and denial.

He realised instinctively that this discovery was going to take him somewhere; he was experiencing a powerful feeling of anticipation deep inside. But he also had a degree of apprehension that swirled around like a black hole, eating everything in its path. Like some menacing gobbler in a computer game.

This was trouble, as much as it was exciting.

The picture of the dragon was somehow connected to the box. For some strange reason, it kept pulling Martin back to it. As did the text he had just read. It was as though he had been reading something familiar, something enticing.

Only when Martin was outside, down the ramp and picking up speed, did he have a horrible thought.

There was no one to tell. Just as there had been no one for some months now since … .

He so badly wanted to stop thinking about the box; right now! The more he thought about it, the more he imagined it might bring him nothing else but trouble – being a paraplegic made him stand out enough; there was no way he was going to jeopardise his chances of being accepted at school, or by his friends, by sharing what had happened with the wooden box.

But he also knew that keeping it inside was beginning to worry him; eat him away – share, don't share – the conflict swirled around inside his head until again and again he imagined it was going to burst. But whom could he talk to?

There was always Dominika, his closest friend; and he

thought about all the times they had shared; especially after the accident. He felt he could trust her. But something had always held him back; a thought, a creepy feeling made him doubt whether he should be telling anyone at all. And he couldn't understand why.

Martin looked down at the sidewalk and realised his wheelchair had come to a standstill. Magnus was staring at him quizzically.

"Sorry, boy. Let's go ..."

And Martin accelerated as fast as he could towards home: number 153 Atlantic Drive, and straight towards a destiny he could never have imagined possible. Not with all the books he had read; all the hours at his computer might he have been able to picture what lay ahead.

But as he raced home, he realised that whatever journey he was about to begin, it had all started with the wooden box.

The box that was no longer buried under the old oak at the bottom of the garden.

::: two :::

A Visitor

suaviter in modo, fortiter in re
gentle in manner, but resolute in action

The garden was somewhat of a problem for Martin. Even when the grass was compacted and newly mown, he found it difficult to travel across it. Often he had taken a tumble, and was forced to leopard-crawl across the lawn. Even though this seemed like the obvious way to go for someone who doesn't have the use of their legs, it was unbelievably difficult. Getting back into his chair alone and on unstable ground was sometimes a very frustrating experience.

The first time this had happened, Dominika had come to visit. He could remember the day well. He had been so self-conscious, he had felt like shouting at her to go away, but had suddenly burst out laughing when she discovered him. The two of them had sat on the grass and laughed and laughed, without really knowing what it was they were laughing at.

There were many times he wished he could walk again, and this was one of them. He made his way across the lawn, to the right of the blooming hydrangeas and the cement path. Thank goodness! It was smooth and wide enough for his chair.

His mother was always saying she wanted to connect the path to the house, but she never got around to it.

Why hadn't Dad done it, Martin wondered. What a strange thing to ask, he realised. How could Dad have known? But it was just this that had begun to worry Martin. He had been having strange thoughts, and equally strange things had been happening around him; even involving Magnus. Martin shook his head, trying to concentrate his efforts on getting to the bottom of the cement path.

Martin loved this part of the garden. The house started to disappear from view, and the path itself curved left, then right and eventually ended in a heavily shaded spot; so covered in fact, that when it rained gently one was completely protected.

It was the place of the old oak.

Martin lent back in his chair and looked up; he found himself nodding and shaking his head almost at the same time. Yes, he realised: it *was* very similar to the one in the book.

He looked down, as he had done so many times before, and his eyes fell on the exact spot of earth he and his father had dug, in order to bury the box. Now covered, and almost overgrown, it had been almost a year since Martin had recovered it. It had taken another six months before he had actually opened the box itself. Before he had had the courage to do so.

14

And that's when the trouble had started.

Martin's father had been a special man. A professor of History, specialising in the two World Wars, he also took a keen interest in Archaeology and had introduced Martin to a wonderful world of books, knowledge, intrigue, fantasy and world events that read even better than some of the wildest adventures on Martin's bookshelf. What Man had done! – the vicious, terrible stuff of war and occupation; and the brilliantly cool stuff of discovery and invention. His father's name had also been Martin; not something strange at first, but only when Martin had grown up did he realise that he knew no one else with the same name as their father; it had made him feel special.

They had had a great relationship, doing so many things together – especially camping! His father would take him to all sorts of places; sometimes to digs where students spent endless hours carefully uncovering ancient ruins, and artefacts. Although Professor Martin had never said so, Martin suspected that's where the box had come from.

It had been after they returned from one of their trips. His father had called him down to the garden one night. He could picture the scene perfectly and hear his father's voice clearly.

"Won't you come down to the tree, old chap," he had said after supper. Martin had almost forgotten his father's request and had been in his room, when he heard his father calling:

"Master Fields! Master Fields, the professor has need of you." Martin had looked out of the window. His father, the tallest man he knew, stood on the edge of the shaded, protected area, at the end of the cement path, where they had built a bench out of stone, and laid large railway sleepers with ground-cover growing in between them; that beautiful, secret place where the ground cover grew ferociously and where everyone in the family went when they wanted to be alone.

That night the Moon had been strong and, from his window, Martin could see his father's balding head shining brightly, itself like some beacon. He waved and his father must have seen him because he waved back. For some reason, Martin could remember every detail of what he had seen from the window, although now thinking back, he realised he must have immediately gone outside to be with his father.

There had been a slight breeze; very gentle. Some of the overhanging branches had been swaying from side to side, as though in slow motion. His father – a giant himself, forever swaying as he walked. Some of the prancing light from the Moon had caught the shiny leaves of the oak tree also, and around Professor Fields, they formed a protective shield or cloak.

Martin sighed. He could feel a tear well up against his

16

cheek and he fought to get rid of the memory. But it wouldn't go away.

He also remembered, so well, his father's mood – he had been even more gracious than usual, his gentle nature coming to the fore, as though drawn out by some ancient moonlight, then shining on them both. But there had also been some tension; some fear. Martin had been just a little afraid; an emotion he seldom felt with his father.

In his hand Professor Fields had held the box. Martin had noticed it immediately as he walked down the path towards him. The moonlight, striking the edges of the box itself – the frame he had so often, since then, lovingly polished and rubbed, as though it were some magical Aladdin's lamp. His father had stood, now rock solid against the backdrop of the silvery light, his head still shining, an almost pale smile on his face.

"I want to show you something," he had said.

Martin held out his hand, automatically, and without hesitation. Now thinking back, he wondered what had given him such confidence; surely he had hesitated, just a little? he now wondered. But the memory was all too clearly etched into his mind.

The box had a strange texture to it, oily, without being oily; perhaps lovingly restored or polished with shoe polish. On its cover he read the inscription he knew so well now.

He had read the Latin, looking up after each word to watch as his father smiled down at him reassuringly. And then his father spoke.

"You'll make a great scholar, one day, Master Fields. Do you know what it means?" he asked.

Martin shook his head slowly, mouthing the words yet once again.

"It means, *it is foolish to fear what you cannot avoid*, his father said slowly. They are words of great courage and meaning. I found it ..." His father had hesitated, and then must have changed his mind because he began another sentence. "It has been a great treasure to me, and I want us to bury it beneath the old oak."

Martin had stared at his father blankly, not knowing what to say. Professor Fields had turned around, beckoning Martin to follow him and crouched at the foot of the tree where he had dug a hole in the soft brown earth.

"I want to bury it right here," he had said. "One day it will belong to you. Right now it belongs here where no one can claim it."

Martin had pushed his arms down and repositioned himself in his wheelchair, so that he could see the patch of earth more clearly.

It was covered up now, the box in his room, in another secret place his mother had not discovered. Small tentacles of grass and ground-cover were growing on the surface, hiding the evidence of the once secret place that had hidden the treasure.

His father had taken the box from him. Just then the Moon seemed to have grown in intensity, and a flurry of wind gushed across the upper branches of the old oak, so that he and his father had both looked up in surprise. Martin had shivered, and remembered placing his hand on his father's knee, as he had so often done as a small child.

"Are you alright?" his father had asked. He had nodded.

"*Are you alright?*" It was *another* voice. Another voice? thought Martin. No only the calming, soothing voice of his father was what he heard right now, almost two years later.

The oak moved again, shaking as it had done that night. There was no moonlight, but dusk was thick in the air, and a faint pink sky filtered through the leaves, making them look like faery lights. Martin sat upright again.

"Are you alright? Are you alright?"

It *was* someone else.

Martin swirled around, loosing his balance, and his wheel-chair toppled to one side, almost sending him crashing to the ground.

"Oh, ssshhew! You terrified me! What are *you* doing here?" Martin almost shouted out each word, and then steadied himself in his chair. He slumped down from relief.

It was Dominika.

"I'm sorry, what's the matter ... what are you doing here?" Dominika put her right hand on the arm of his chair, her voice anxious and a little afraid.

"Oh, nothing. Nothing. I just ..." Martin looked at her in a slight daze. "Dominika, strange things have been happening. I really need to tell someone, but I just don't know who to turn to. Mom won't understand. I went to the library, and this book. Oh, shew! There it was – a picture in this ancient book; I mean this book about ancient ..." Martin wasn't making any sense and he stopped to gather his thoughts.

"Don't you want to go to your room and tell me all about it?" said Dominika. She was ten months older than Martin, and they had been almost inseparable since meeting. It had been another strange event some five years before. Martin's father had introduced the family to a 'very distant' cousin from 'far away', three times removed, although neither Dominika nor Martin had ever understood who was removed from whom, and why any *removal* had taken place!

20

Why had he never told her about the box? Had it been fear of what his father had said, of the inscription? Now, out here in the semi darkness, under the cover of the great oak, Martin could almost not believe that he had kept it all a secret for so long. Perhaps he had not wanted Dominika to get involved; perhaps he had been mindful of the words in the inscription – the thought of wanting to avoid something. This could surely only mean that something terrible was about to happen.

Perhaps this thought, and the thought that he didn't want to hurt his friend, had forced him to keep quiet.

And then he remembered that he had opened the box only just a few months ago. And what with school, and starting his racing program on the track with other athletes; perhaps there just hadn't been time.

But all the same, it now seemed strange that he had not told her.

He looked into Dominika's eyes, almost as if to say sorry. And then he shook his head.

"Yes, let's get out of here. It's kind of spooky. I do have something to tell you and I hope you've got time to listen."

"Sure," said Dominika. "Dad is having a barbeque with some friends and I don't feel like meat, so I told them I'm staying over with you tonight. Glad I came; clearly you need me here!"

Martin was smiling again, and boxed her gently on her arm.

It was going to be a moment they would both remember for the rest of their lives.

Once inside Martin got out of his chair and onto his bed. He was still debating how much to tell her; whether to show her the box or not, or to simply tell her what had happened.

"Do you remember the camp we had at the lake? The one where you caught all those spiders and teased me with them?" (Martin hated spiders, and they were Dominika's favourite). Dominika nodded.

"Do you remember me telling you about a secret – I got you back for frightening me with your spiders by not telling you…?"

Dominika raised her eyes towards the ceiling and nodded. "Yes, I do remember something like that – but that was …, it was …"

"Yes, it was just before the accident, about three weeks before," said Martin. "Well, my Dad and I buried a secret box under the tree where you found me earlier."

Dominika nodded slowly, and her eyes widened, showing increased interest.

"Well, it stayed buried until about a year ago. I dug it up, cleaned it, and …".

"And …?"

"And, well, I didn't open it for some time. I was afraid. My father told me that I would dig it up one day and would open it at the right time."

"And you didn't know if it was the right time, or not," added Dominika, helping Martin out and showing that she understood. It was why they were such good friends and why Martin liked her so much; she was able to read his mind at times, and really understand him. He was beginning to feel better already.

"I eventually did open it. I think I did the right thing, but sometimes I'm not so sure."

"Why?"

"Because strange things have been happening …"

"For instance?" asked Dominika, leaning a little closer to him.

"Well, for one thing, Magnus."

"Magnus? He seems fine, doesn't he?"

"Yes," said Martin, "he's fine, but about a day or so before I dug up the box I found him sitting beneath the bench where Dad used to sit."

"So?" said Dominika, not fully understanding. "Perhaps he misses your Dad too, you know." She was beginning to sound just a little impatient.

"No, you don't get it; it's as if Dad was *there*. Magnus was looking up at *him* on the right side. Dad only ever sat on the right, always leaving a place for me. Even if he was alone, he always sat on the right hand side, just below the sweeping branch we used to climb to the tree house.

And...well, he was sitting looking up with his head cocked to one side. It was as if he was listening to someone – to Dad. He never goes down there alone, not without me, even when I'm not here – you can ask Mom. He lies in the sitting room, or in my room and waits for me, but never down by the tree. Not until now, anyway."

"Okay – so what we've got here is a dog that misses his master and sits waiting for him to..." said Dominika and stopped short of finishing her sentence.

"Yes," said Martin, "as if waiting for him to come back. I've never told anyone about this. But he wasn't just sitting there – he was pawing the air and actually *talking* to Dad, just like he used to. He never talks to me like that – you know the way he jumps up onto my lap, or licks me, or barks. But he never talks, not even now. He was talking to Dad! I know it, I could feel it. And the weird thing was he didn't even notice me until I called him; and even then I had to call him three times."

Dominika looked blank. She wanted to see what Martin was seeing, but to her nothing seemed really strange at all.

"And that's not all," said Martin. "His seat was warm."

"Whose seat was warm?" Dominika usually picked up on everything but this time missed it.

"Dad's seat on the right hand side. I can't explain why I did it, but when Magnus wouldn't come to me I went over there, lent over and felt the stone bench; it was icy cold except for Dad's side. I could really sense him there."

"I suppose that is a little weird," said Dominika.

"That's nothing. Now when I go down with Magnus, or even sometimes without him, his place on the bench is always warm. I'll show you sometime. And I can always sense his presence, as if he's...he's telling me to do something."

"Like what?"

"Like, well, I think that's why I dug up the box. I felt it was the right time because he told me to do so. I felt good about it, like I always do when I go down to the bench. There's more."

"More?"

"Lots more," said Martin. "Dad's laptop ...

There was a sharp knock on Martin's door. "Do I hear the voice of someone I know?" asked Martin's mother in her usual playful tone. She was very fond of Dominika and they shared many secrets together.

"It's me, Mara," answered Dominika – she had always been glad to have a substitute for a mother.

"Well now, aren't you lucky; just in time. Having meat for supper again?" asked Mara with a smile on her face.

Dominika burst out laughing. "I hope you don't mind, but I'm starving," she said.

"Mind? Your room is ready if you want to stay. And I've got just the thing for you: red peppers stuffed with anchovies mushrooms and savoury rice. And of course sausages for Martin. Perhaps a little voice told me you were coming?"

A little voice? Dominika and Martin looked at one another.

"You don't have to look so serious, you two. Come on, supper's ready. And there's pudding too!"

Martin lifted himself into his chair and allowed Dominika to push him to the table. She was the only person he allowed to do this, unless he was in trouble.

The meal was great, but for a reason Mara couldn't fathom, they were quite eager to finish.

"Can we please take our pudding to my room, Mom?" asked Martin as soon as he dared.

"Got some secrets to share, have you?" said his mother,

cocking her head to one side, just like Magnus.

Martin and Dominika glared at each other.

"Okay, off you go, you two. I've got some work on the computer anyway. Dom, you know where your bed is. And your toothbrush is in the bedside table – the mauve one I bought for you last time."

"Thanks Mara. Thanks for the food; it was great!" said Dominika, as she rose from the table.

"Yes, great, thanks Mother Dear," echoed Martin.

Back in their room, Martin looked at his friend. "Do you think she knows?"

"Knows what?" asked Dominika. "You haven't convinced me of anything yet. Now hurry up, eat your pudding and out with it. Now!"

Martin smiled. It was always great to know more than Dominika did; she was the Dux at school in every grade, but this time she would have to do most of the listening.

"Even the computer – the way Mom said the word. It's as if she knows."

"Knows what!? You're driving me mad Martin Fields, and I'm about to tattoo your arm with my knuckles, if you don't hurry up."

Martin lowered his voice, "I've got Dad's laptop, as you

know. And I use it every day. But at least twice a week I switch it off. Every time when I come back to my room, it's switched on – I asked Mom about it; she doesn't do it, and I trust her when she says that. But not only is it switched on, there's a screen saver I can't find anywhere. It's the inscription on the box, in Latin. Here let me write it for you …"

"Why not just show me on the computer?" asked Dominika.

"I told you I can't find it anywhere; it's only when I come home sometimes after switching it off, and boot the computer up again."

"It must be somewhere," said Dominika. "Have you clicked on Browse to find images?"

"You should know better than to ask that – I know every jpeg, every screensaver and every image on the laptop, my computer and on Mom's. You're forgetting computers is the only subject I manage to beat you in. Do you really think…?"

"Okay, okay," said Dominika, admitting defeat. "So, when you come back, after switching it off sometimes there's this inscription."

"Yes. And as soon as I use any program, it disappears. Here it is in Latin." Martin had written it out for her: *Stultum est timere, quod vitare non potes.*

"Okay genius – translate. So what's it mean?"

"It means, it is ..." Martin pointed to the word *est* ... foolish (stultum) to fear (timere) what (quod) you cannot avoid."

Dominika looked pensive for a few seconds. "And that's a direction translation."

"The last few words actually mean, not (non) able or possible to avoid."

"Mmm," said Dominika. "That's pretty cool; and that's on the cover of the box?"

Martin nodded. He was looking down, as though sad again, perhaps just thinking. "But that's nothing. In fact all I've told you up to now is quite innocent. Perhaps you're right about Magnus. Perhaps even he was sitting where Dad used to sit and he made his place warm. And Mom's little references and looks. Perhaps that's all explainable." He shook his head again, in disbelief, in fear, perhaps. "There's something else very weird."

Dominika craned her head forward as if to say, *okay, okay?*

"It's inside, inside the box that the real scary stuff begins." Martin took a deep breath. Dominika lent even further forward:

"Uha, uha! I like it ...!" she began to sing. "Come on, out with it!"

Martin shook his head as he blew a lung full of air out

29

through his lips so that he looked like an old man snoring. "I don't know, Dom; perhaps I should just bury it again and all of this will go away…"

"Oh no you don't, Master Fields. I've been around long enough for you to trust; remember I'm family. In fact I'm tired of this nonsense. Get the box now, or I go home and tell everybody at school you lost some of your brains in the accident too."

Martin looked up in astonishment. Dominika suddenly felt guilty and she lent forward to put her arms around her cousin and give him a big hug. She had tears in her eyes when she pulled away. "Of course I won't; it's just that you're driving me *crazy* with this stuff. Please get the box. Pleeeeeezzzzzz!!"

"Okay. It's up there." Martin pointed to the top of the cupboard.

Dominika jumped off the bed like a flash and stood in front of the double doors.

"Hang on a minute … how did you get it up there? I can't even reach!"

"Ahh, that's my little secret. Just open the top cupboard and take down my sleeping bag."

Dominika stood on a chair and did as she was told. It was bulky and deformed looking. "Clever little mite, aren't you? And you reckon Mara hasn't found it yet?"

"I doubt it – she's hardly going to look inside a rolled up sleeping bag now, is she?" said Martin.

"I suppose not. But how did you get the bag up there again?"

"You forget, I'm not the under-twelve javelin and discus champion for nothing. There nothing a good aim can't solve," said Martin chuckling out aloud.

Dominika opened the sleeping bag carefully on the bed and out popped the box.

They sat silent for a moment, staring at the beautifully carved wood; the inscription, just as Martin had said, stood prominently on the top. Dominika tried her hand at mouthing the words and almost got them right. Martin patted her on the back in praise.

"Now, let me open it," said Dominika.

"NO!" Martin shot the word out. Dominika recoiled in fright. "Sorry – before you do, you have to hear this first." He took another deep breath as he repositioned himself against his large pillow. "When Dad buried it that night, it had a note inside with just one word written on it: 'Tantalis."

"Tantalis," repeated Dominika.

"Yes, just one word". Martin spelt it out: "T a n t a l i s."

"What does it mean – the name of someone?"

31

"I don't know. Dad didn't say. He just folded it up and placed it inside the box, and then buried it straight away."

Martin took Dominika's hand. They looked at one another, both feeling a little uncomfortable with the physical intimacy. He had never held her hand before.

"Okay, now you may open it slowly."

There was a sudden knock on the door.

They both stifled a scream; Dominika tore her hand away from Martin's and shoved the box under the bed covers.

They were both breathing heavily when Mara peered round the door.

"Everything alright in here? Things are awfully quiet, you two. No more pudding?"

"Just fine thanks," they both echoed one another. "We're just sharing the usual secrets!" added Dominika. Mrs Fields chuckled to herself and closed the door again.

This time it was Dominika who took the largest and deepest breath before she recovered the box.

"Okay, let's do this together," said Dominika. "You and I. At the same time. Each one with one hand on the cover. Ready?"

Martin nodded.

Slowly, as though they were expecting some terrible thing

to come leaping out, they opened the box. There was no sound, no creak, no hinge that got stuck; just a smooth action until the box was fully open.

Dominika peered inside, her long, wavy-wild curls hanging down so that they touched the soft, dark wood.

She looked up at Martin. "There's a key," she said.

Martin nodded slowly. "U-huh," he said slowly, "a key."

Dominika gingerly took it out. It was quite large. The kind of key one found in an antique store. It looked as though it was made of silver, or perhaps pewter (although neither of them would have known this). The handle was beautifully carved in the style of the wrought iron one finds on the verandas of old Victorian houses. This both Martin and Dominika recognised because there were many such homes in their area.

"So, it's a key …" said Dominika.

"Yeesss …" Martin motioned with his hand as he so often did with Dominika, egging her on to see something else. Dominika looked at the key again, once again pensive; silent.

"Oh! You mean, where does it fit?"

"Yeess, but that's not it…remember what I told you about the night we buried the box…". Dominika thought again.

"Oh, you mean you didn't say anything about a key. And …"

33

"Yeess – go on; no key but …?"

"But …" Dominika was really trying hard this time. "No key, but, but. Oh, you mean, where's the note?"

"Ha! You got it!"

Dominika wiggled her nose from side to side.

"Let's see if I get this straight. Your Dad calls you down to the bottom of the garden one moonlit night, the wind's blowing; the moon's shining on his bald head." They both began to giggle. It was probably the first time Martin had remembered his father with laughter since the motor car accident itself.

"Come on, be serious," he said between chuckles.

"Okay, okay. He shows you the box; lets you handle it. He reads the inscription – stultus, something – don't fear…whatisname …, and then opens it to show you a note. On the note is the word *Tantalis*. You both close the box. He tells you that he's going to bury it and that you should only retrieve it one day when you know it's the right time. This is a little spooky because, because …" Dominika lowered her voice a little and said the words slowly, "because it's almost as though he knew he wouldn't be around when you did..?"   "I never said that; but looking back, that's exactly how I felt," said Martin, sadly.

Dominika continued: "He buries it. The next week or so at the camp you tease me about a 'secret'. Nearly a year later, after

34

you've recovered from the motor accident, you start to think about digging it up, which you do. But you don't open it. How'm I doing?"

"Pretty good so far," said Martin.

"And then …" Dominika trailed off, losing track of things.

Martin continued: "I dig it up; take it out of the plastic bag – I think I forgot to tell you that. Keep it up there for about six months because I'm too scared to open it and because I'm training, etc. Then one day…"

"You open it," finished Dominika. "And inside is the key without the note!"

"Yes," said Martin, triumphant, "you've got it!"

"The box doesn't have a keyhole, and you haven't taken the key out of the box or tried it anywhere."

"How do you know?" asked Martin.

Dominika looked at him funnily. "You would have said something by now, surely."

"Okay, that's it. Too afraid; didn't know what to do. I mean, where do I try? It's too big for any door I know," he pleaded.

Dominika was silent for a long time, now and then shaking her head. Eventually she said: "well, we must assume it fits some door, or something else; otherwise what's the point, right?"

"There's no door around here, at least I don't think so," said Martin. "But then again I haven't tried."

Dominika looked at Martin, got off the bed and stood in the middle of the room. Martin didn't have to ask what she was thinking, and he pulled his wheelchair closer to the side of the bed and manoeuvred himself swiftly into it.

"We'll just have to see," said Dominika. "Let's first make sure your mom's in bed." She peered down the passage and noticed a thick beam of yellow light beneath the door of the main bedroom. "Okay, let's do it," she said.

She pushed him around the house, from room to room, the key hidden in Martin's lap. There was nothing in the kitchen, and certainly nothing in the sitting room – no door, no box or container they could see, or think of. Dominika knew each corner of the house as well as Martin, and she was as puzzled as he was.

Suddenly they heard a sound from the bedroom.

"What's all that scuffling about?" called Mara, from her bed.

"Ah … nothing, just taking a tour of the house," said Dominika.

Martin looked at her wide-eyed, and whispered, "that was a *real* lame one."

.

Dominika shrugged her shoulders deeply, as if to say, what else could I have said?

"Okay – hope you find something exciting!" called Mara, going back to her book.

They both looked at each other blankly.

No luck. They found no place for the key; each lock was a modern one and neither Dominika nor Martin could think of anything old that might fit. They returned to Martin's room and back to his bed and the box, a little disheartened.

Much later that night when Mrs Fields peered around Martin's door, they were both asleep, Dominika's head resting on Martin's large pillow at the foot of his bed. She seemed to be clutching something under her right arm. Martin was in his usual place. What great destiny had brought these two together? she wondered, as she closed the door gently.

She walked back to her room slowly, glad of the peace and quiet. When she sat down on her bed, her gaze turned to the portrait of her husband – how easy it must seem to others, she thought, to be jolly, to appear to be coping well and making the best of things.

She touched the picture with her right index finger and tears welled up in her eyes. But how difficult it had been, though; and she could not make up her mind whether she might have shown Martin a little more of the grieving that swirled inside of her daily. She thought she heard a noise outside, but simply wiped her tears away, and then lay down hugging the picture against her chest.

Outside, a few branches in the old oak gave a slight shudder.

Had Martin and Dominika been anywhere near, they might have looked up and noticed there was something moving in the tree house above the bench.

::: three :::
A Beckoning

inter nos
between ourselves

This time it was Dominika's turn.

The next day after school, it was she that was standing at the bottom of the garden, looking up at the old oak, when Martin wheeled himself over the lawn and onto the path. She was so engrossed she didn't notice him at all; only when he was right behind her did she spin around in marked surprise.

"Phew! Now I know how you felt the other day; that was scary," she said.

"How do you mean scary?" asked Martin.

"I was almost somewhere else just now, and you kind of pulled me back. I don't know why I was surprised, because I heard you, but just couldn't pull myself around."

"Where were you?"

Dominika paused. "I don't know, really." But she pointed half-heartedly to the tree itself. "I was there, I mean here...it was strange and at the same time enticing; as if something was calling me."

"Now you are beginning to know what I mean, because

that's how I feel when I come down here. Perhaps that's how Magnus feels too," said Martin.

"Hmm," said Dominika, "there's something there; someone, something. And the funny thing is, when I was staring at the base of the tree just about where you took the box out, I felt scared, but only until I remembered the inscription. Suddenly I thought about it, and I felt calm. Kind of reassured, so to speak…"

"You mean it has some, some power. Or, rather, what you're saying is that it gives you confidence …"

"Yes, that's it. I could even remember it as though I had learnt it just like you, and I haven't ever done any Latin at school," she said. "And I've been thinking about the key," Dominika continued.

"So have I," said Martin in surprise. "What did you come up with?"

"No, you first …"

"No, you. Okay – I am wondering whether it is more of a symbolic key than an actual key, like a key that opens a lock somewhere – we've been looking all over and can't find it. I wonder, maybe it's telling us that our situation, or something we have, like the box itself, or maybe even the tree; maybe they are a key in themselves…"

"Exactly!" said Dominika grabbing the side of Martin's chair. "Or maybe, and listen to this: maybe you and I are part of the key! What do you think of *that*?"

"Wow – I like it; it kind of makes sense," said Martin after a while, although not entirely sure what that might mean. "Where's Magnus?"

"Magnus? I don't know," said Dominika impatiently, "why worry about him?"

"Because I haven't seen him all afternoon."

Dominika suddenly seemed to focus, and came back to reality suddenly. "I'm sure he will turn up. Listen, I've got to go. Cheerio Old Chum." She was smiling, remembering that this was what Martin's father often called him.

And then she was gone, leaving Martin alone at the foot of the old oak. As if to acknowledge his presence, the tree gave a gentle sigh as a breeze caught its branches.

Magnus appeared later that night, in Martin's room when he was preparing for bed. He seemed to beckon Martin, wanting him to go outside.

"Where have you been, you silly dog!" chided Martin. "Don't be silly – I can't go outside now. I have to put my catheter in and finish some work. Go on, settle down and be quiet."

But Magnus was not wanting to settle down at all and ran

41

from Martin's room.

In fact, if Martin had taken him seriously, if he had just believed him enough to only look out of the window, he might have seen something quite strange.

Until late in the night, just as Martin had related to Dominika, Magnus could be seen pawing the air as if in conversation with someone. But there was no one to see him.

Or was there?

The week came to a sudden end, as often weeks do. It was Friday, Martin's favourite day and he was due at the gym for a special workout with his team-mates for an upcoming race. He was starting to take his upper body seriously, and he had a special programme as well as swimming which he enjoyed the most.

He liked the fact that the pool was reserved at special times for other paraplegics, so he didn't have to feel self-conscious about swimming. He wore a floater which allowed him total freedom of upper-body movement. In fact it was only in water that he felt totally free, just like everyone else, even though he could use only his arms to move around.

When he got home, his mother was waiting with a message from Dominika.

"She had to go to a school function with her Dad, but says she's coming around afterwards to sleep over."

"Okay," said Martin, not feeling like much more company. In fact; he was particularly tired and could think of nothing better than one of his mother's meals in front of the television. "What's for grub?" Martin bent down to acknowledge Magnus and give him a scratch behind his large floppy ears.

"Grub? Master Fields, after such a day, you expect me to make you grub?" said his mother playfully, "How about beef and tomato stew with flavoured aniseed rice and freshly steamed garden peas?" She watched him closely for a reaction, knowing this was one of his favourites.

"I'll take a long shower and imagine how good it's going to be ..." said Martin disappearing down the corridor and smiling to himself.

Magnus followed him in earnest and growled gently behind the curtain while Martin positioned himself in his chair under the warm spray of water. If only he could talk, thought Martin.

The supper was wonderful, as always.

Magnus, for once, was at rest at Martin's feet, and the television tuned to Martin's favourite channel: Discovery.

Before long, Martin found himself drifting off to sleep; somewhere in the back of his mind he was aware he should stay awake for Dominika. Perhaps it was the programme about

43

mummies that bored him, perhaps just pure exhaustion, but his head kept on dropping onto his chest.

Later, he caught his mother lifting him from his chair into his bed.

"Sorry, Mom," he said as he helped her move his legs.

"That's alright, darling. You're exhausted. Shall I send Dominika home when she comes?"

"No," said Martin thick with sleep, "let her stay. We'll get up early tomorrow morning. I want to go to the library again with her …"

"Okay, you get some sleep now …"

She said something else, but Martin was gone, far away, into a land of inscriptions, dragons and ancient artefacts; the main feature of his dream, no doubt, was a small, but sturdy and beautiful box with a key inside.

The key. It was always the key that featured in his thoughts and dreams these days.

Martin woke with a fright. The room was dark and some-one was shaking him gently. He tried to focus, hearing his name being called, but he was so drowsy that he battled to fix his eyes on anything except a looming outline.

He fought to loosen himself from its grip, and even called out, "Go away. Go *away!*" But the thing persisted. And then he could hear a voice that was familiar. It was Dominika's.

"Martin please wake up. We must go. It's Magnus; he's at the foot of the tree again, pawing ..."

"Oh, *please* go away Dom. I just want to sleep ...," said Martin, now almost fully awake. "What time is it?"

"It's about a quarter to eleven," said Dominika.

"What are you doing here?" asked Martin.

"I've come to sleep over, don't you remember? But I'll go home, if you don't want me," she added in a tone that showed a little hurt and a hint of frustration.

"Okay," said Martin pulling himself up to a sitting position with some difficulty. "So what's new – you want to chat; couldn't it have waited for tomorrow? I've been training all afternoon, and I can hardly sit up I'm so tired."

Dominika suddenly felt guilty. "I really am sorry, I mean it. But when I got here and had some grub with your mom, I noticed Magnus was missing again, so after supper I looked out of the window, and there he was, doing just what you described. It was really .... really kind of compelling. I couldn't take my eyes off him. I reckon something *is* going on, and I think we should go down there ...", She didn't have time to finish.

"Now!?" said Martin, incredulous.

"Yes, now ... remember that stuff you said about us *being*

the key, and the box and the key itself, and perhaps that the tree is also some kind of key, or link. I've been thinking about it all day. And I think we're both right. And what's more I think it's more than coincidence that we both had the same thoughts. I think we should go down and see what happens." Dominika was almost out of breath, she was speaking so fast.

"Okay," said Martin, convinced. "But I do think we can do this tomorrow morning."

"I don't think so. No. It's now. I can feel it," said Dominika almost desperately. Martin sighed, his eyes closed in final acquiescence.

He put on a thick jumper just in case it was cold, and then on second thoughts, his track-suit pants also, while Dominika looked the other way.

"What about shoes?" asked Dominika.

"Oh, that's really funny," said Martin. "What do I want *them* for?"

"I don't know," said Dominika sheepishly, "but maybe your feet will get cold.

"Okay, you can put them on; they're over there." Martin lent back in his chair while Dominika slipped on a pair of socks and his sneakers.

'There, you are. You look cool."

"I'm not sure I want to hear that."

"Come on," said Dominika smiling, "it's a compliment from a girl; you're going to be looking for them pretty soon."

"Yeah, yeah ...," said Martin, feeling a little embarrassed. "Where's Mom?"

"She's in bed and the light's off. I checked."

"You'd better get the key, if you want to try something spooky, " said Martin, with a tease in his voice. Dominika reached up into the cupboard, retrieved the sleeping-bag and took the key out of the box.

She wheeled Martin expertly through the house, the living room and out onto the porch; the one small step onto the lawn was easy, but she had to leave it up to Martin to negotiate his chair across the grass.

Sure enough Magnus was sitting at the foot of the tree. Just like both Martin and Dominika before him, he seemed not to notice anyone behind him, and whirled around suddenly when they were both right next to him.

"What now?" asked Martin.

"I don't know. I guess we just sit quietly," whispered Dominika, "and see what Magnus does."

It was dark.

Through the leaves and branches of the old oak, Martin

47

could see faded lights from the town beyond, twinkling. And what had become a customary feature, much like a greeting, the branches began to move gently from side to side, breathing, as though reacting to some force; something out there that was more than simply a breeze or wind.

Magnus was motionless, every now and then he would lift his left front leg, and paw the air, pointing towards the tree and also the bench where Professor Fields had so often sat.

Martin shivered slightly, partly because a cold chill gripped him and also because he was beginning to be a little afraid.

He instinctively held onto the large key in his lap, allowing his right hand to grip it somewhat tightly. Just then he remembered the inscription on the box, and without fully realising it, whispered the words, "*Stultum est timere, quod vitare non potes.*"

The tree shook violently. Magnus let out a sound that was a half bark-cum-grunt. Martin could feel himself free of his chair and he grabbed the arm rests instinctively. A gust of wind seemed to almost tug at them and Dominika grabbed onto Martin's shoulders, to steady them both.

Suddenly they both felt a cold rush of air hit them full in their faces. The soft, gentle twinkle of lights went out, and there was utter darkness.

Thump! They had fallen, or landed somewhere.

But how could they? They hadn't gone anywhere. Right in front of them was the old oak, but without the sparkle of lights shining through the branches.

"What was *that*!" said Martin.

"I don't know; and why is it so dark?" asked Dominika.

Magnus was on his feet, wagging his tail, as if to say, Yes!

"Oh my! Look at you!" said Dominika with a look of shock and pleasant surprise on her face, although Martin could not see her clearly.

"What!" said Martin full of fear, whirling around.

And then it hit him.

He was standing!

"Oh, my *word!*" He moved one foot, and then the other. He could walk!

He let out a squeak of delight and began to dance around. The old oak in front of them remained quite still until Dominika noticed something.

"This is not your old oak. At least, it looks like it, but...Martin. Martin, stop," she said urgently. "We're not in your garden."

Magnus was sniffing around at the foot of the tree.

"I can walk," said Martin, "this is crazy." When he had had

49

enough of staring at his feet and legs, touching them, slapping them, and kicking them about, he looked around.

"Did you hear me!" said Dominika anxiously. "We're not in your garden."

"Well, if we're not in our garden, and I can walk, there's only one explanation; it means that we're dreaming, which means I have to go back to my chair...speaking of which, where is it?" said Martin looking behind and next to him. He groped the thick air, but found nothing.

"It's back in the garden, at the foot of the tree, I suppose," said Dominika, also looking around.

"Well, shall we go back?" asked Martin, now a little calmer, "it's very dark out here, and I'm not sure I like it any more."

It was not just dark, but very dark. The air was thick with something, like a mist or cloud, and it felt as though something was pressing in on them; perhaps just thick foliage, thought Martin hopefully. He sniffed the air; there was a smell that was quite foreign; decidedly foreign. He knew what it was like to visit strange places and always, on each trip with the family or his father, he had remarked immediately on the smell of the place. This was dank, only just stopping short of being unpleasant; a very slight chill in the air, and no light to speak of.

It was what he had often, as a child, imagined some dark

50

forest to be like – when his father had read from books on my-thology and fantasy. He began to shiver, his legs now wobbly.

"Perhaps you're right," said Dominika, "at least I hope so; if we're not dreaming, we're in trouble."

Martin didn't let his grip on the key loosen for one second; still in his right hand, he followed the ornate carving with his in-dex finger, up its shaft and as far as his finger would go. Once again, he found himself uttering the inscription. This time Dominika detected his whisper, and copied him, although she didn't quite get it right.

There was a muffled scuffle.

It sounded like it came from the right of the tree, and through some undergrowth.

The dank smell grew stronger. Dominika stopped reciting the inscription abruptly, and whispered:

"What's that?" said Dominika. Magnus turned his head too, moving forward. He was wagging his tail, then stopped, un-sure of himself. He uttered a gentle, soft growl, and then just as quickly stopped. His tail resumed its seemingly joyful dance.

Then there was a voice:

"You're not dreaming. Oh, no. You're not dreaming at *all!*" The voice was husky, thick with age, purpose, and just a little menace.

51

A smallish figure appeared.

Both Martin and Dominika lurched backwards into each other's arms, groping, bumping one another off balance.

"What are ... who are you?" shouted Martin, with Dominika uttering a quiet stammer at his side.

Martin steadied himself and strained to see through the darkness. The figure loomed, and then clearly a face. Yes, a face it was, but an ugly one – gnarled features, protruding cheekbones, a high forehead punctuated with perfectly round, smooth growths. Perhaps it was just their imagination, after all it was dark.

Suddenly the figure flicked a switch and a light appeared. It was the creature they had both imagined, in flesh, and right before their very eyes. It spoke again, this time with a hint of a smile:

"Hello! Just in time." And then it uttered a strange sound which would become its hallmark, and which sounded something like: "OoOoooo-ee; **yess**." It stepped forward, obviously wanting a better look at both of them.

"I think I want to go home now," said Dominika, clutching Martin, and almost whimpering.

"Not before we find out what's happening," said Martin, wondering where the sudden surge of courage had come from.

52

"Well now. You can if you wish, but we've been waiting for you. A very long time, a very long time." He lowered his large head slightly, tucking his chin into his chest, and moved it from side to side. He seemed to be brooding, contemplating.

"You can go back, but will you *come* back? That is the question. It's been a long time waiting, for us, for all of us…"

"Okay," said Martin, now with even greater courage. "We'll go back when we know who you are…"

"Mark this tree," said the face, lifting its head and turning towards the oak that looked just like Martin's old oak. "It's a marker; they all look the same. All are portal-havens, and often some are none."

"That's all we need," said Dominika, still shaking a little. "A spooky figure talking in riddles."

What's really got me puzzled is why Magnus is not barking, thought Martin, too afraid to speak his thoughts out aloud. Magnus was still wagging his tail, but with much less intensity than before.

"Why? OoOoooo-ee; **yes** …" said the figure. "Who I am – my name Trollip; and … Magnus," he said, noticing Martin's gaze, "well, we … old friends, you know. Introduced by someone else, by …." He trailed off, squirming slightly, with a look of apprehension on his face. Martin could just make this out in the

53

soft light which emanated from the lamp-like instrument he held in his hand. "Ooo; mustn't say, mustn't say; sorry. No names. You'll see. You'll know. When the time is right."

"You're not making sense, " said Dominika, now having regained some of her own courage; and then added, "I don't think…"

Trollip laughed, a guttural, deep, puckish laugh. "It's you who have to make of this. It's definitely you. I can see now." And he shone the light into the faces of both Dominika and Martin. "Yes. You'd better come with me."

"Come with you? You've got to be joking," said Dominika. "We've come too far already. Besides, I've…I've got to be back tomorrow; got to go somewhere important. I'd better go right now, thank you." Even though she was trying not to be frightened and spoke with confidence, Martin could see that she was not having a good time.

"Suit yourself. But perhaps you don't know how to go back, and Magnus and I have something really important for you to see," said Trollip, adding his little strange sound at the end.

"Martin, let's just go back. Hold up the key; hold it up and face the tree; *please!*" Her voice was almost desperate.

Without objecting Martin held up the key.

But what happened next really surprised them.

Trollip fell to the ground, holding up his hands, mumbling, mumbling, calling out and groaning in some language neither of them could understand.

And Martin felt a renewed strength. He felt it in his legs, in his hands and arms; he felt it in his whole body.

But most important of all, he felt it in his heart.

For some strange reason, he didn't want to go back.

Not quite yet.

::: four :::
Trollip

medio tutissimus ibis
a middle course will be the safest

Trollip was not impressed. "Must be *careful* with that …;" he said, still holding up his hands, "not for us, not for meee, not my business … don't want it near meee; it's given to *you*. You listen to it. Don't do that, don't do that!" There was a plaintive tone in his voice. It was almost as though it was afraid of what Martin held in his hand.

Martin opened his hand and looked at the key, and then at Dominika. What power did this key have, he wondered; and why was this creature so apprehensive about it?

He raised his eyebrows and shrugged his shoulders; at least they had some advantage over this creature, especially if he turned out to be bad.

Trollip had regained his composure and placed the light on the ground; he beckoned for them to sit around it which they did, sheepishly, still not sure whether they could trust him. Magnus sat down also, looking from one to the other, licking his lips, his tail gently wagging behind him.

Trollip rubbed his enormous nose. Both Martin and

56

Dominika lent backwards slightly, as though expecting something to come out of it. He was not a pretty sight, with large growths all over his face, and thick hairs growing from deep inside his ears. His eyes were small, and black with a piercing centres, acting like some super accurate laser beam, each time he looked at them.

"You make up your mind now? You come with me. I'm here waiting for you, and I been sent to fetch you. You bring the...the..." he pointed to Martin's hand.

"The key?" said Martin, making as though to hold it up.

"Yes – keep it safe," said Trollip backing off. "It's not for me, not for me." He pushed a long, gnarled finger into the top pocket of his waste coat and pulled out a black object which he put in his mouth. He began to chew, his eyes rolling slightly from side to side.

"Ohhh, OoOoooo-ee; Yesss!" he said, "*much* better, much better; nice ....," he said smiling.

"What is that?" asked Dominika.

"Ohh, an olive ... an olive," said Trollip in a lilting tone, "a special one for meee," he chuckled. "Now look here; here," he said bending forward with a stick in his hand. He placed his left index finger into his left ear and dug around while he spoke. Dominika grimaced.

"Here we at a portal-haven tree. " He drew a dot in the

57

earth, and both Martin and Dominika lent forward in the bad light to see. "We on edge of the Dark Woods, which is good. It's good. But it's not. Because dragones cannot see us, and we need them ..."

"Dragones?" asked Dominika, looking a little frustrated, "what are *they*?"

"Ohh," said Trollip, looking surprised, "they our friends. Trollip taking you to Phantoam, chief dragone (*pronounced dragoan, or dra-gone, or dra-gonè*). He tell you all the little bits and pieces. That my job, you know, because they trust me and I have sword!" Suddenly he pulled out, from nowhere it seemed, a short thick, menacing sword and swung it in the air; the paltry light only just enough to make it visible in the darkness. Both Martin and Dominika fell backwards.

"Shew! I *wish* you wouldn't do stuff like that," shrieked Dominika.

Trollip smiled wryly. "You keep the, the .... and I keep my sword tuck away; tuck away!" he said, and as quickly as he had drawn it, he made it disappear behind him. Dominika looked relieved.

He continued: "Now, we must travel through the Dark Woods, which is good. But also not, because dragones cannot see us ..."

"You've said all that," said Dominika. Martin nudged her, motioning for her to be more patient, but Dominika was not keen to listen. "I don't want to do this; I want to go back," she said, her voice whining slightly, which was so unlike her.

"Oh, *that's* a good one," said Martin indignantly, "this was all *your* idea, remember. I was perfectly safe in bed, now because of *you*, I'm stuck out here without my chair, my catheter and with this, this fairy-thing ..."

"Oh! Not! Not *nice*. Oh goodness, goodness ...," said Trollip in astonishment. "I not, not a faery. Faeries are others, others."

"Okay, okay – I made a mistake," said Martin holding up his hand. "Sorry. But *can* we get on with it. We really need to know where we are; and you speak about showing us things. Can you just tell us what's happening, where we are ...?" He looked sideways at Dominika, lifting his eyebrows and shoulders, although nervously, yet trying to give her some assurance that he was still on her side.

Trollip started all over again but neither Martin nor Dominika wanted to stop him this time. They were careful not to make any sudden movements or to ask any questions.

It seems they were on the one side of the Dark Woods, and like most adventures and fairytales, they had to reach the other

59

side; except the smell of Trollip, the size of his sword and the eerie presence of the Dark Woods made their experience very real, and *not* fairy-tale stuff at all.

Neither Martin nor Dominika had managed to bury their doubt and fear enough for them to gain a sense of adventure or purpose. Yet. Although they were largely intrigued, they reacted to Trollip much as though he were some disliked teacher at school – but one they had better listen to, or else. In the back of their minds, they both relied heavily on the hope that holding up the key against the old oak would take them straight back home. And so they found themselves in this strange place, and yet not yet committed or serious about going further. One could not blame them; their emotions ranged from sheer fright, to extreme apprehension, doubt, uncertainty, and without any of the familiar cues they normally found in their daily lives.

But this was no faerytale, and they had seen no faeries.

Trollip was more than just serious about his mission, and had they known what waited for them up ahead, they might have jumped back into their garden, buried the key forever, and gone straight back to bed, never to mention a single word of their encounter to anyone.

But they didn't know.

And perhaps this was why Trollip wasn't telling them too

much.

"We must go now," said Trollip. "You follow me, closely; must be quiet. Magnus knows; he knows to walk quiet."

Magnus *knows!?* thought Martin.

"You must be qui-eeet." Trollip stopped speaking, reached into his pocket again and popped another *special olive* into his mouth. Satisfied with this action, he started to walk, looking back to see whether they were all following. Martin looked back at Dominika, raised his eyebrows once again, cocked his head to one side, and motioned for them to follow. She shook her head but got up and walked behind him.

Trollip had a strange gait. He loped, his body moving from side to side, a little like a gorilla, yet this didn't seem to diminish his agility at all, and in fact he was somewhat difficult to keep up with. Every now and then he would stop, lower his head, cock it, and listen. If Martin and Dominika were making any kind of noise, he would raise his hand to silence them. Satisfied they had stopped, he would continue.

It was very dark, but by now, even though Trollip had extinguished his light, both Martin and Dominika could make out shapes, and even textures in the brush. It was a thick forest, sometimes menacing in form, often beautiful; and at least some light, perhaps from a Moon, filtered gently, like a soft brush, through the leaves of the trees and down onto the floor of the forest. Martin sniffed the air every now and then, recognising a slight change. They were now much deeper, and although the original smell of the forest was ever present, his nose told him they were approaching something new.

Dominika called from behind in a harsh whisper, "so what are you, if you're not a faery?"

Trollip continued his loping scurry, "I'm a troll!" he said proudly. Dominika simply couldn't contain herself any longer and let out a loud shriek of laughter:

"A troll called Trollip! – my goodness, how on earth did we miss that?!"

Trollip stopped abruptly, causing Martin who was not yet steady on his feet to crash into him, and Dominika into Martin, and Magnus into her. Wham! Magnus winced and then sneezed loudly, shaking his head.

"No! Not funny; loud noises, no … *please!*" he said turning around so that his great nose almost touched Martin's cheek. "Must, *must* be careful with your noises; can give us away. *Please* no."

They all backed off to a more comfortable distance.

"Give us away?" asked Dominika. "Pray, do tell whom you are talking about!" She made herself sound as though she were on stage, reciting the lines of a play, and Martin began to giggle.

"I'm talking about ... about." Trollip made an attempt to lean closer for them to hear him. Of course they backed off even more, afraid of his looks and also of his bad breath.

"Just whisper, quietly, and not so *close*," said Dominika, in a forced whisper herself. Trollip looked a little hurt at first, but then a twinkle came to his eyes and, a little like a child, he said:

"We must look out, look out. There are others; faeries are good, always good. No bad faeries. And of course trolls; good trolls, but look out for bad ones ..."

"You mean you're a good Troll but there are also *bad* ones?" asked Martin.

Trollip raised himself right up as far as he could go. "Of *course* there are bad trolls," he said indignantly. He almost barked the words out too loudly, but caught himself just in time. "Bad trolls, just like bad *people!*" He pushed his nose towards them, as though to remind them where they had come from. "Bad people, too; also bad trolls. But no matter, they scared of Trollip, because of my *swooorrd*." He made as though to retrieve it again, but Martin held up his hand quickly, stopping him.

"And, and then there are the ..." Trollip looked distinctly sad. Half cringing, as though in anticipation of defeat or loss of some kind, he said, pregnant with meaning, and with such terrible menace that he shuddered, "the In-quishhhh."

"The *what!?*" asked Dominika, almost laughing at this new revelation.

"Shhh ... shhh," said Trollip, still half curled up, but also looking from side to side. "Not laughter; they can hear laughter, because they know humans. Know humans. They smell you, hear you, but not me. They are; they are bad bad, **bad**!" He lent very close, beckoning them to come near, and lowered his voice to an almost inaudible whisper, "the In-kwish ..." he said, phrasing each syllable separately.

He looked at them quizzically, and continued very slowly, as though both Martin and Dominika were really stupid, "many Inkwish, one Inkwa!" he said, letting his head fall backwards with a little triumphant, loud whisper.

Dominika blew some air through her lips gently, shaking her head at the same time. "These are the bad trolls?"

She had clearly said the wrong thing.

Trollip flapped his hands up and down against his thighs in frustration, "Oh ... oh! No! Goodness me, goodness me, you *not* listening to Trollip. Not listening. Trolls are trolls. Inkwish are Inkwish." And then he drew in his breath quickly, and covered his mouth. "Bad to say name; they hear me like they smell you, when I say name. Not *again*. You *not* ask again, you understand?"

Martin and Dominika nodded, and looked around, feeling decidedly unqualified to recognise or deal with these new daunting revelations.

Martin began to feel that perhaps Dominika was right. He was feeling the pull of his warm pillow back home.

Besides, as much as he felt delighted at the sensation, his legs were beginning to ache.

Trollip turned to resume his journey and then stopped suddenly. "Oh silly troll," he said, "silly, silly; the ...." He turned around to whisper again, "the bad trolls ... they can maybe see you in the dark. Silly Trollip. OoOoooo-ee; yes. Must cover faces! Cover with mud. Here," he said bending down and retrieving from the ground, as if magically, some mud, "put it over your face. They must not see."

"Oh, gross!" said Dominika, touching it, "it's slimy and stinky!"

"Don't suppose we have much choice," said Martin, "better do as he says." And he took some of the mud from Trollip's hand and smeared it directly onto his face. After some protesting, Dominika allowed Martin to do it for her.

They continued slowly. Trollip in front, loping gently; Martin behind, followed by Dominika and then Magnus, who was quite content to be the last. They walked this way for at least one hour, until Dominika began to complain and make Trollip nervous, so he stopped.

They were on the verge of some clearing and Trollip pointed to an enormous tree ahead. It was much lighter now, but neither Martin nor Dominika could make out if this was some kind of dawn, or a more intense moon, or simply because they were now in a clearing.

When they reached the tree, they found it was largely hollow. Martin stood erect, and let his head fall backwards to view the full extent of the tree's height, but it was impossible; they were too close, it was too dark, and the tree itself was simply too big.

They entered. The slight chill in the air disappeared immediately and a fresh smell appeared; strangely neither dank, nor musty, nor that of a tree rotting. It was almost a sweet smell; a welcome one at least. But then perhaps the tree was not rotting at all, and Martin sat down on soft crumbling bark and rested his head against a piece of gnarled wood. The inside of the tree was large enough to accommodate them all comfortably.

Trollip sat down at the far end and, strangely, Magnus lay down next to him, wagging his tail and raising his head each time Martin looked his way, as though to say, *yes I still love you, but this is the best guy to be near right now; please don't feel bad.*

Dominika sat right up against Martin, also glad of the covering, protection and soft ground.

"It's weird," said Martin.

"Weird? What do you mean?" said Dominika. "Weird is *normal* out here; weird is your life in the last while, what could possibly suddenly be weird?"

"Dom," said Martin softly, loosening his grip on the key and placing his flat hand on her arm to comfort her, "you're the weirdest of all. *You* are normally the positive, courageous one; after all it was you who got us here, remember. I came to you with all of this, because of *all* the people in the world, I expected you to be able to give me support just as you have always done. What's wrong?"

Dominika shook her head, and tears began to well up against her cheek. Martin felt both sad and warm inside; he felt he was able to give her something of the strength and comfort she had so often offered him, but at the same time it made him feel a little silly.

And then two things happened. It suddenly occurred to him that his own courage and strength, especially in such an abnormal situation, was unusual, and perhaps came from somewhere else. He handed the key to Dominika and bent down to massage his legs. It was a strange phenomenon, the taut muscles, aching as they had done years before. And then something else happened.

"Oh, my word!" he said out aloud. "I want to wee!"

"Thanks for that," said Dominika, sarcastically.

"No, you don't understand. I don't have a catheter, and I can feel that I want to wee. You know how long that's been?"

Trollip came forward. "Not wee here! Must wee outside in mud; not wee against tree like Magnus; they smell men; smell *you*."

"This is the Inkwish, you're talking about," said Dominika.

"Oh, no," said Trollip. "Inkwish don't come in Dark Woods often. The bad trolls; they smell you; they tell Inq....; you know. Come with me outside; I look first; to see if all clear."

Trollip knelt down, peered outside to sniff the air with his head cocked, and then motioned to Martin. He found a patch of mud, not far from the entrance to their hideout.

Martin weed with glee, almost calling out aloud; he felt he wanted to sing. It was both strange and familiar at the same time, being able to actually feel the urine flowing from his body. As Dominika had said, everything was entirely weird.

When he got back Dominika was looking much better; in fact a new-found calm permeated her face entirely.

"We've been overlooking the obvious all the time," she

said quietly to Martin as he sat down next to her. "It's the key. And I think the inscription, too."

"What about them?" asked Martin sleepily.

"They both give us strength," she said, allowing it to sink in.

At first Martin didn't react, and then he remembered the journey so far. "Of course!" he said. Trollip looked up, uttering something they couldn't understand, and Martin continued more quietly: "They do; every time I've held on to the key real tight, I've felt better, my legs especially. And also when I've said the inscription, I've felt even stronger. In fact calmer...the fear has gone away."

"That's the key, so to speak," said Dominika, proud of her pun and also of her discovery. She definitely was more herself, thought Martin.

Just then there was a swooping sound: loud, yet muffled. Almost deafening. Martin and Dominika ducked instinctively, their hearts beating suddenly, caught somewhere between their chest and throat. Trollip sat up abruptly and looked upwards. It lasted for just a few seconds and then went away. All was quiet again.

"OoOoooo-ee; Yes," he said, with his usual tone, and popped an olive into his mouth. Martin and Dominika looked at him quizzically, waiting for an explanation.

"It's a dragone ... goooood. Yes, goood," he said, "looking over us; he is watching. Knows where we are. Always good to have dragones flying over ..."

"Yes," said Dominika, "you haven't finished telling us – you said something about Phantoam, the chief dragone and that he would tell us 'bits and pieces'."

"Phantoam – chief dragone. I must take you there; he wants to see you."

"What are they?" asked Martin.

"You don't know dragones? Not good, you don't know. Phantoam told me you know dragones ..."

Martin looked at Dominika, "you mean dragons?"

"No, OoOoooo-ee" said Trollip, "dra-*gones*. Great, big – they fly above us, and sit council with elves. Veeeeery wise; very wise; tell stories to trolls; trolls *loooove* dragones. We work for them and the faeries."

And then Trollip became sad; he buried his head in his folded arms and began to sob, so that eventually his whole body shook. Soon it was almost a wail, which he tried desperately to silence. The tears streamed down his cheeks, and Dominika felt quite sorry for him. He managed to continue: "Man killed dragones, so many of them, so they ... they; that's when we became Tantalis …" And he began to cry loudly again.

Martin looked at Dominika, "Tantalis? You mean – Tantalis – that's where we are?!" He almost shouted this out.

"Yeeess …," said Trollip, sobbing gently this time.

"But why are you crying? What's wrong with Tantalis; is it a bad place? Why does it make you sad?" asked Martin.

"No, Tantalis good place, not sad for Tantalis," he paused slightly, regained himself, wiped away some tears and with his hand on Magnus's head continued, making them even more confused than before: "Tantalis not proper place. I'm sad for dragones." He drew himself up slightly and peered at them, a little accusingly, "Man killed dragones, not good, not good. And we went back, went away. Bad men." He stopped and then seemed to grow quieter and more composed, "just like bad trolls," he said eventually nodding.

Soon he had another olive in his mouth and was smiling again.

Martin shook his head. His mind was raging. The inscription, the key, the box. Tantalis itself – the word etched in his mind so clearly: he could see it written on the paper inside the box. So they were in Tantalis – the very place his father had told him about, inside the box. This alone made him feel better; closer to his father, his memory.

71

"Let me see if I can remember some stuff," said Dominika looking at Trollip, "you don't like the key, it makes you nervous, but Martin must hold on to it tightly, because he must do something with it. There are trolls, good and bad, fairies who are only good and whom trolls work for. Dragons or dragones, that fly over and watch us safely. Inkwish which are bad, bad, bad (Trollip recoiled at the sound of this), and the tree we met you at is a safe portal." She paused, looking at Martin. "Oh yes, and we're in Tantalis: a place? And we're going to see Phantom, no … Phantoam, the chief dragone who will tell us 'bits and pieces'…?"

Trollip stared at them blankly; Martin looked at him and then at Dominika, raising his eyebrows slightly as if to say, *so did we get it right?* But there was nothing forthcoming from Trollip. He simply rolled over and made himself comfortable.

Within seconds he was asleep, leaving them both staring at him blankly.

In the dead-quiet and hush-still of the forest, they could detect a soft, gentle sucking, much like that of a baby suckling.

It was Trollip, with the remainder of an olive pip, which he sucked quietly for the rest of the night. And that was the end of him. At least for now.

::: five :::
The Lair

pro patriâ
for our country (fatherland)

Martin woke with a start; immediately looking around. Trollip was awake and standing over a very small fire in the middle of the hollow. Magnus was sniffing at the entrance; Dominika still asleep.

Martin sighed, but was not sure whether it was from relief at finding they were safe, or from the uncertainty and uneasiness of the previous day.

Part of him wanted desperately to be back home; it was clearly morning and his mother would be calling him by now. Part of him wanted, of course, to continue to wherever they were going. The fact that they were in Tantalis had made it difficult for him not to want to know more and go further.

Slowly the details and discoveries of the day before began to flood his thoughts. He groped for the key, and found he was still clutching it. Perhaps the last discovery: that they were in Tantalis, had made him realise that they were where his father wanted him to be.

That in itself was comforting. And it was a comfort that

would sustain them both, again and again.

Dominika woke. Martin put his hand on her shoulder to ease her back to the reality of their situation, managed to elicit a thin smile. Her thick mop of hair hung wildly around her face, and for the first time Martin felt a mild sense of affection for his friend – she was not only his companion, his challenger and his fan; looking now at her he suddenly noticed how pretty she was. She looked up at him, and then her head moved slowly across to Trollip.

"What are you doing," she asked.

"Food; making food," said Trollip, proudly. "Good trolls can cook; good food. Bad trolls..." He pulled an ugly face and dismissed the thought with a wave of his left hand, the index finger of which he immediately stuck into his ear.

Dominika pulled a face.

There was a small fire, and only one large glowing coal, once a log; above it, suspended in a neat contraption, was a large leaf – the kind one would imagine from a tropical forest – it was folded over and raised above the fire just enough for the heat to cook whatever was inside. Martin could see heat and steam rising gently from the sides of the folded leaf.

When Trollip scooped the contents into small hard bowls, they were all hungry and ate the food with relish. It was good, and tasted of wild herbs, with a sweet meaty flavour. Martin held the bowl in his cupped hand and realised it must be some kind of large seed pod; they ate with sticks, neatly carved into eating utensils.

"Did you do all this?" asked Martin, lifting the bowl and stick; "did you make this now?"

Trollip continued to eat, and eventually replied, "this is troll hollow, safe portal too. Always things to eat."

"I'm thirsty," said Dominika.

"I'm worried about time," said Martin. "Shouldn't we be waking up at home now? What happens if they don't find us there?"

Trollip shook his head. "Still sleeping sound," he said, "back home, you still sound sleeping. Don't worry, Phantoam will give you all bits and pieces to understand. We must go now," he said taking the bowls away from them, swiftly wiping them clean and then stacking them in a recess in the tree behind him.

Outside the sun filtered through the thick forest canopy; it was quite beautiful. They didn't have to walk far before they found a stream, and once Trollip had cleared some undergrowth away, they all bent down to have a long drink. The water was especially pure and sweet, having just minutes before surfaced from deep within the earth somewhere above them, up a hillside

75

they could not clearly see. They continued on their journey.

Neither Martin nor Dominika recognised any of the trees; not that they were experts, but they knew enough to realise they had probably not encountered them before. There were few oaks – the majority were softer, with thick, smooth bark and trunks, their branches fanning out widely. Above them were taller trees of a completely different kind.

Trollip walked around each one he encountered with respect, pausing as if he might be able to hear or smell something; perhaps they were each portals of a different kind; perhaps he could detect something from each one separately, as though they were markers on a map. Either way, his reverence and care caught their attention each time.

There was no direct light or sun at all, and they understood why Trollip had spoken about the dragones not being able to spot them.

"Why was there a dragone last night?" asked Dominika, "I thought you said they couldn't see us."

Trollip remained fixed in his loping gait. "Dragone can sometimes see portal-haven trees; dragone knew where we were last night. Chasing bad trolls away; bad trolls very frightened of dragones' wisssshh above…" He pointed above him, and they both recalled the sound of the previous night.

"How are your legs?" asked Dominika.

"Oh, they're fine; only a very slight ache. I suppose it de-pends how far we have to walk," said Martin, once again remem-bering the key and giving it a good stroke with the flat of his hand. When he had finished, he handed it to Dominika and told her to do the same which she did. She soon spoke: "I suppose we can only see this as an adventure; we've got nothing to lose. If they discover we've gone, then we've gone." It looked as though she was regaining confidence as much as she was looking for confirmation in Martin. He stopped to take the key back from her and smiled, "As always, Dom, you seem to sum things up just perfectly. I couldn't have done without you these last two years, and now I'm really glad you're here also."

Her hair was still as wild as it had been when she woke up, and a slight breeze caught the wispy strands and flung them up-wards like candyfloss. Martin gave his own hair a cursory brush with his one hand, trying to find the parting.

Magnus was obediently and patiently walking next to Trol-lip's side, looking back now and then. Perhaps he had learnt his lesson from walking behind them all, when they had all collided.

They followed the stream; Trollip stopping to listen, it seemed, to the sound of the water itself. Martin noticed they were upstream and climbing. Soon there was a partial clearing and while Trollip ventured into it, both Martin and Dominika lurked behind. "Come, come," said Trollip.

"What about bad trolls?" asked Martin.

"No bad trolls in day," said Trollip. "Look." And he pointed directly above them, through a clearing in the canopy – probably less than the space of a large picture. High in the sky, they could make out a shape – larger than a bird, much larger, with short stubby wings and a huge body, although it was almost impossible to judge because they were not sure about the distance, and this made comparisons difficult.

"We being followed ...," said Trollip smiling. "Now we climb a little; up, up there." He pointed through the thinning thicket where a hillside was clearly visible. "Coming to the end of the Dark Woods; remember Dark Woods, safe in the day, and portal-havens safe at night. Remember." He watched them as he spoke, making sure this had all sunk in. Both Martin and Dominika motioned that they had understood.

The Dark Woods was kind in that it offered no sudden ending; it waned gently, until just a few trees punctuated a steep hillside. Large boulders positioned themselves decoratively across the landscape, some large enough to carry a crowd of people, or whatever creatures lived in Tantalis. They were a light grey, with varied fungus and lichen growing all over them.

In fact the scene was quite soporific and both Martin and Dominika found themselves feeling quite sleepy, basking in the brilliant sunshine as they entered the gentle climb.

High above them, at what appeared to be the summit, a cluster of trees beckoned them; one clearly looked like an oak but Martin could not be sure in the sharp light. Instinctively he knew they were making for them.

Suddenly from behind a boulder to their left a creature leapt into view, shrieking: "Kagaaa ! - Kagaaa ! – kagaaa ! Phissssterisssss!"

Martin and Dominika fell to their knees in fright.

Trollip, in a flash, whipped his short sword from behind him and threw it with such speed at the creature, that neither of them could detect its path in the air. It landed with a 'shoekkk!' in the ground, right at the creature's feet. The creature froze – no sound; not a single movement.

It was clearly some kind of lizard. A long curly, but sturdy tail seemed to prop its body in a very erect position, so that it looked at them with a haughty and menacing stare. It could not have been more than half a metre tall, and although Martin could detect no movement coming from it once the sword had landed in the ground, he could clearly make out the thumping of its heart in the creature's upper chest region.

His own heart began to beat in unison, banging against his ribs, and he opened his mouth to clear what felt like a restriction in his windpipe.

Dominika had gripped his left arm, and it was beginning to throb.

Trollip burst out in vile and loud expletives, although in a foreign language. When he had calmed down a little and had retrieved the sword, he held the lizard-creature up by its neck, and said: "Goodness, goodness – silly thing; Trollip thought was little, baby Inq … ." Once again he motioned with his hand for them to understand they should finish the word; Martin made a sound to show that he understood.

"This not baby; silly thing, full of bad talk, full of naughty…but not…; I let him go now." And with that he let it drop to the ground. It hissed at him, now seemingly free of the spell or sheer terror of Trollip's sword, and scurried off up the hill, not turning once.

Trollip chuckled, probably less at the antics of the creature, than at his own reaction.

They were soon half way up, and the sun was beginning to press them with the sheer weight of its intensity. Magnus was slobbering, his tongue hanging this way and that in an attempt to cool down.

Trollip turned around and pointed with his hand outwards over the top of the trees below.

In the distance, mist. To the right more hills, undulating into mountains – could they see snow on top? Martin wasn't sure. The forest itself extended far into the distance, and they understood why it was difficult to see inside – the canopy of leaves assured a thick covering.

And then it caught their eye.

Once again high above, but not as high as before, flew what Trollip called a dragone. Even though the sky was empty, and he had nothing to compare it to, Martin could clearly see that it was huge. They all stopped. It looked quite different from conventional dragons he had seen in books. Not a little unlike the one he had seen in the library.

"Look," he said to Dominika, finding that trying to speak with his head thrown back hurt his windpipe and made the sound funny. The sun was a little sharp so they had to strain to see. Its head stuck out clearly, with a long protruding mouth that formed a clear silhouette against the sky; its body was bulky, in fact larger in comparison to Martin's understanding of a dragon. It definitely had wings but, strangely, these were small, and thin. They could see feet, legs and even front paws. Its back arched up towards its tail, and all along, ridges like a crocodile or dinosaur –

that part seemed to fit the picture he had always carried in his mind or seen in drawings.

It hovered, more than flew, began to rise in the air, up, up and then simply became a dot against the sharp light of day.

"We must hurry," said Trollip. "Phantoam waiting for you, for me; waiting for me. I get prize," he said proudly. Magnus barked for the first time, perhaps in anticipation of something he already knew.

They climbed further; it was now getting to be unbearably hot and Martin's legs were aching again. He clutched the key, this time both hands rubbing it until he felt better, remembering the inscription as he did so.

Suddenly they came to a crack in the hillside, invisible from below; Trollip paused to wait for them, and then entered. It was barely large enough for them to fit, but they did so without having to walk sideways. Up ahead it looked dark, and within minutes of walking in the cool air inside the hill, Trollip switched on his light. He was unable to lope and seemed to move with some difficulty.

Deeper and deeper they went. Eventually there was no light at all, and they were feeling their way forward. Only the scuffle of Trollip's large bony feet and the occasional noise from Magnus gave them some bearing.

"Not afraid," he said, "don't be afraid – come, come; nearly there for the prize!"

Just as they began to shiver from the cold, a warm, yellow light filtered down the thin corridor of the passage; the passage itself widened, and they found themselves at another entrance. When they worked their way further forward they could see, over Trollip's short body, that it was a large cave.

Trollip kept quite still; Magnus at his side, now and then looking back at Martin and Dominika.

Martin clutched the key, and could hear his heart beginning to pound as it had done before. Dominika, afraid to take his hand, perhaps, held onto his arm. They both looked around.

The cave extended high into the hillside or mountain. Above, small droplets of water formed, hitting the ground near them when they dropped. It was rocky, with many curves, crevices and protruding formations of stone, some making interesting and colourful shapes. The smell. It was pungent, old, somewhat airless, and had a toxic edge to it that made them hide their faces in their shoulders to protect their nostrils.

Trollip said, "stay here; you stay here." Neither of them were going to make any move whatsoever. In fact, as interesting as the cave was, it was also new, also foreign and quite frightening, and their instinct was to retrace their steps, and head straight back to the Dark Woods. But there was a tone in Trollip's voice that made them clearly understand they were not going to be able to do so.

He moved deeper into the cave with Magnus, bent down and picked up a small object that seemed to shine. He said something, but not to them and in a language they could not understand. And then just as quickly and mysteriously as he had appeared the previous day, he disappeared with Magnus, around an outcrop of overhanging rock, into a lighter and broader passage to the left, and was gone.

They were alone.

The only sound was that of their hearts climbing desperately, it seemed to escape from their chests.

"This is not cool," whispered Dominika softly into Martin's ear. He pulled his head aside with fright, even though her words had been just a whisper. "I don't like the faerytale, dragon stuff; they can keep this for books. Now I *do* want to go home."

"We're in Tantalis," said Martin, trying to instil some confidence into her; but as much for his own sake, "I know it's scary, but we've got each other, and I'm sure this is where Dad wanted us to be." This time he took her hand and held it tightly.

Just then, from against the one side of the cave, there was a shifting and scraping – and even without being able to detect its source, both Martin and Dominika knew instinctively that the sounds were made by something, or someone big. Something really huge.

It spoke.

::: six :::
Bits & Pieces

ex longinquo
from a great distance

They both strained to see where the sound was coming from. And then as though switching on a light in a darkened room, their eyes were suddenly opened. Both Martin and Dominika shrieked from the sheer terror they felt, when it came into view.

"Aahhh!" Dominika shouted and whimpered at the same time, her voice quivering.

"Woe! WaaHH!" Martin clutched a protruding rock and Dominika at the same time, falling backwards.

They both found themselves on their butts in the dirt.

The far side of the cave was more the creature itself than anything else; it had blended in so well, they hadn't noticed it at all.

It was clearly what Trollip called a dragone.

Now each detail, each colour, and more noticeably, each pungent smell was clearly discernible, and filled the cave around them. Its body, huge, curved as they remembered seeing that morning up in the sky; all the way down to its tail, spiked arches, like some gigantic crocodile. The tail curved right around its body, thick at the joint, and thinning to a point at the end. Its body was bloated; perfectly round in the belly, and fading from the almost peachy orange above, to a creamy-white deep beneath it where its body lay on the floor of the cave.

It spoke. So as not to frighten them further its head moved slowly, down in a swing-like motion towards them so they could see its face. The eyes were almost human. Ancient, and somewhat tantalizing; large, somewhat piercing, and in the centre of the arctic white, a deep, clear sea-blue neither of them had ever seen before.

"You'd better move towards the side entrance and get some air." Its voice was controlled and deep, and rich in tone and texture. It was nothing like Trollip's. Here was a voice of authority, perhaps even wisdom, and as they would both soon find out, a voice they would be able to trust.

"I'm glad you finally made it. Trollip always delivers; or at least he usually does, when he's concentrating. See anything bad? Bad trolls, perhaps?"

Both of them shook their heads from side to side, wide-eyed, not ready to engage; still afraid.

"I am Phantoam – Trollip told you about me? I know I must be scary. Man has forgotten who we are, what we look like.

87

Your books have only waning memories of real dragones. You saw Acktare in the sky above you outside?"

They nodded; whoever Acktare was, they were not going to make any enquiries about him just yet.

"I'm glad; he can be troublesome, sometimes. He's still in training. Now, you are Martin and you are Dominika," he said, allowing his great head to descend towards them. His body followed behind, almost shaking the entire cave.

They recoiled, trying to push themselves into the rock behind them.

"No – don't be afraid. Stultum est timere, quod vitare non potes, remember!"

"You, you know! – don't fear ..." Martin began.

"Know?" said Phantoam, "it's what keeps us going in Tantalis." He chuckled deeply, his voice carrying a hint of sadness and just enough mirth to make them feel better. He settled down again, his great size shifting the dust on the floor of the cave.

There was still the toxic smell, coming from Phantoam, or at least deep within his lair, and they turned towards the entrance and light to take a deep breath of the fresh air that blew gently towards them.

'Yees, that's it; always take a deep breath away from a dragone," said Phantoam, chuckling again, "we don't exactly have much in the way of sweet aroma, at least not to a human nose."

He shifted slightly again, "Of course trolls don't mind." He closed his eyes as though a little weary, "My goodness, apart from … I don't think a human has smelt a dragone's lair in over a thousand years.   And of course, even when we lived together…mmm, I don't suppose humans had the need to come into our lairs."

'You don't remember?" asked Martin bravely and without his voice faltering.

"Oh, no. I'm not quite a thousand years old. And so I can only surmise, imagine. No, there would have been little need. We visited them; even ate with them; hence the great halls and castles that Man built; they weren't just for showing off, you know. But then, the Inkwish. Oh dear. Our alliance broke off as I am sure Trollip told you. And everything changed, now here we are pinning our hopes on the two of you; or at least you, Martin, to bring it back again…"

Martin looked at Dominika with raised eyebrows, pulling his lips back against his cheek as if to say, *me? What do they want me to do?*

Phantoam seemed to be in a deep reverie, and regained composure only when Martin spoke.

"Trollip didn't tell us very much, and we have lots of questions, but we're really worried about going home. We need to do things back home this morning; and my mother will be looking for us right now." They were still quivering slightly.

"Oh, no. You're quite mistaken. Believe me its still the dead of night back there. You can count on at least one day for each hour gone from your home. In fact there is hardly any correlation between time here and there; you might even return and find you've lost no time at all. But no fear; you can leave at any time, from any portal-haven; you should know where to find them by now...?"

"Well, not really, Trollip didn't point out too many; we slept in one and entered through one, but I'm not sure I could find one," said Martin, trying to breath normally, in between each phrase.

"Oh yes, you can. You can already recognise the old oak – they're all over the place. On the edge of every clearing in the Dark Woods are portal-havens. And the others you will instinctively know about, when the time comes."

"I'm glad you're confident..." said Dominika softly, making sure she didn't look Phantoam in the eye.

"I like you," said Phantoam, cocking his head towards Dominika; "you're a little bonus, so to speak. We didn't expect you." He lifted his head and continued: "Well, we have work to do. But before we get on with it, here is something you might enjoy."

He shifted his huge body sideways, lifted his front leg and dexterously produced a thin gold chain with an exquisitely beautiful gold locket shining brilliantly on the end.

"Put it on, Dominika," said Phantoam. She could hardly refuse, carefully took it from his long, thin claw-like fingers, and put it round her neck gingerly.

So dragones really did steal gold and jewellery, thought Martin.

"Are you hungry?" said Phantoam.

Even if they were, it wasn't something they were worried about right now.

Phantoam produced something that looked like a small chicken; placed it on a grid-like structure in front of them in a recess in the wall, and beneath it placed two or three pieces of wood.

And then he did something surprising; something that made both Martin and Dominika recoil from fright.

He blew gently onto the wood; a clear, sharp, sparkling, thin line of flame, out of his extended mouth, and which ignited the wood immediately. In fact the flame itself was so intense, that it immediately turned the wood to bright burning ambers. Soon the piece of meat was sizzling.

For the next ten minutes or so, Phantoam, paused to turn the meat, otherwise he engaged with Martin and Dominika, allaying some of their fears, conjuring up new ones and trying his best to make them feel at home.

"I still don't understand why Trollip is so scared of the Inkwish," said Martin, now a little calmer, and gazing longingly at the fire.

"Well, they're the cause of everything going bad. Once like proud elves, at least a branch of them, they revolted against the rest of us and formed an alliance with the dark side of Man. You must remember we and Man lived side by side for aeons. In fact, I suppose it didn't even start with the Inkwish," said Phantoam, turning the meat for the last time, and bringing it down so they could reach it. "It all started when Man himself revolted. You see he wanted to be all powerful – the old story – and decided that it would be a good thing to kill all dragones so that the rest of the world would listen to him. Well, he was right. He did kill most of us, and then did take over the world. Except it was without the ancient wisdom he enjoyed before."

Martin and Dominika couldn't wait any longer; even though it was hot, it was so delicious they found themselves sucking in great gulps of air to cool their mouths and the meat inside it.

Phantoam let them eat, watching them all the time, careful not to make a sudden move and frighten them. It grew quieter in the cave. Outside the sun still shone brightly and filtered itself, across forest and glade, touching stone, mountain top and hillside, and finally absorbed by the great sandstone of the side of Phantoam's lair itself into a soft yellowy, spongy light.

"So." said Dominika, eventually. "Man and dragones lived together; the two working together, with dragones teaching Man much of what he had to know, and then one day Man decided to overpower dragones and kill them – he got jealous?"

"Yees, I suppose so," said Phantoam, as though a little sleepy, "what he really wanted was the secret of flight; and when ancient dragones said he wasn't ready for it, this was when the trouble started. And that's when the Inkwish came in. At first, after Man killed most of us, we withdrew – all of us: the Queen and all the Elves, the remaining Dragones, Trolls. In fact the entire 'mythical world'." Phantoam said the word, mythical, with contempt, showing clearly that this was how Man saw them. "Faeries, elves, entire races – we all realised that Man would soon come after us one by one, jealous; hungry for power. If he could kill dragones – his best friend, his teacher and sage, can you imagine what he would do to others. There was no contest. We simply withdrew. And that was when the Inkwish came into being."

"This is really good stuff," said Martin, "What is it?"

"Oh, let me see," said Phantoam bending down, so they could smell his breath, "it's a Phisteriss – something like a water rat, but much bigger than rats where you come from."

"Oh, disgusting! Yugh!!" said Dominika, spitting out some meat.

"Well," said Phantoam, "it was good, wasn't it?"

"Yes," said Martin, "but it's just the idea; aren't rats dirty?"

"Not here; they're especially clean, that's why we eat them. It's a great delicacy for elves. In fact, you're lucky to have one. No one besides an elf gets offered one in my lair!" Phantoam looked decidedly hurt.

"Oh," said Martin, looking at the meat in his hand again, "I suppose we're just not used to it. But it was good." And then after some time realised he was probably eating the creature that had frightened them earlier.

"You were saying about the Inkwish?" said Dominika, putting the remainder of her meat down in front of Martin, her mouth turned sideways in disgust. Phantoam ignored the look on her face, and continued:

"They took sides with men, and conspired to kill us also. And then when we banished Man, or withdrew, they seemed to adopt his, his... well, I suppose one could say, his dark side. They have become evil; most evil. They don't have much sway over us dragones, mind you. Make sure you keep away from them; which reminds me. You have the key?" Phantoam shifted again, and he bent right down to stare directly into Martin's face. Martin hastily dropped his last bone, and clutched the key in his hand.

"Of course. What about it; you know about it?"

"Oh, good," said Phantoam, withdrawing again, "just making sure. It's crucial; don't let it even slip from your hand."

Phantoam coughed and a great gush of fire erupted from his mouth, against the side of the cave. Both Martin and Dominika recoiled in fright.

"Sorry, I need to relieve myself every now and then," said Phantoam. "You can be glad it's not from the other end," he said, chuckling loudly.

"How ... how do you make so much fire?" asked Martin, almost quivering again.

"Well, it's easy, really. I have chemicals deep in my stomach, and when they come into contact with the air, they ignite. Simple." He chuckled loudly, "Man has all but forgotten about dragones. Or ..." Phantoam paused as if to reflect, "it is possible

95

they want to forget on purpose, especially after they did manage to steal the art of flight."

"What do you mean?" asked Martin.

"Well, it's the way we are made; not in any way the same as your faerytale books portray. You can see how big I am. What about my wings?"

"What about them?" asked Martin.

"Their size, said Phantoam.

Dominika started to speak, and then stopped.

"I know," said Martin. She looked at him, as if about to reach the same conclusion. But before she could say anything Martin blurted out:

"They very small."

"*That's* the mystery. In the world of humans, man features dragones, or dragons as they call them, as creatures with large wings; mostly huge in fact. And your scientists, having forgotten the old magic and ancient knowledge, cannot understand how dragones ever flew. They all say, *it's impossible for dragons to fly – they're too large.*"

"Mmm," said Dominika, her eyes narrowing.

"Don't understand," said Martin, eventually after a long silence between all of them.

"Well, it's simple; how can such a large creature fly? is the question they all ask. But it's the wrong question."

"You don't use your wings!" said Dominika suddenly.

Phantoam smiled. Martin was thinking about something else, though.

"Tell us more about the Inkwish," he said, interrupting.

"Well," said Phantoam, "they're almost as clever as elves, cunning; evil at times, and they have managed to manipulate humans expertly."

"Why?" asked Dominika.

"Because, when they realised they could not entirely overcome Tantalis, they discovered the key was humankind itself. Control human beings, and control the world, so to speak. And Tantalis. They slip into the world of humans and manipulate them into wars – both the first and second world wars were precipitated by them."

Phantoam paused, and lowered his head as though grieving. "Such misery; pain and wilful destruction. We dislike them *so* much!"

"So the Inkwish are responsible for the two world wars?" asked Martin, cautiously.

"Yes; but for so much else that the world wars pale into insignificance…"

"Into insignificance?" said Dominika, getting up to stretch

her legs. Dominika could well remember lessons on both world wars – the first so terrible in fact, that she still remembered pictures of battles in which more than half a million soldiers were killed, along with their horses. Some called it the *war to end all wars*. That was how awful it had been, and how people had wanted to remember it. Of course just twenty one years later the whole world was at war again – this time ending with the most destructive weapon Man had ever seen – the atom bomb. She looked at Phantoam, wondering whether to challenge him – how could anything else make these two events pale into insignificance, she wondered.

"They have taught Man terrible things," continued Phantoam. "Hatred of one another; worst of all, hatred of the Earth, and of animals. Pollution is just one example.

Did you know?" and he bent down again to get their attention, "… they even gave humans plastic!"

"Plastic?!" said Martin looking up. "What's so bad about plastic?"

"Yes. This *wonderful* material that promised to solve so many problems. Everything is wrapped in plastic – every new product, from a load of bricks to packaged food, even every loaf of bread in the world today. The world is now full of plastic, with not nearly enough recycling. The sea itself is full of it. It's just a matter of time before human beings do it all themselves."

"Do what themselves?" asked Martin.

"Damage the Earth irreparably. That's the Inkwish's goal – once man has brought about enough destruction, the Inkwish will move in. Probably parading as their saviour!" scoffed Phantoam loudly. "Tantalis was not enough, it's the entire Earth they now want for themselves. And we've *got* to stop them!" said Phantoam with a final flourish in which he flicked his huge tail that had until now been still. It landed with a thud against the side of the cave. Dust from the walls rained down gently on them. Martin and Dominika recoiled again, but this time not nearly as frightened as before.

The sun began to sink slowly and both Martin and Dominika, despite their inactivity for the last few hours, began to grow weary. They were not entirely comfortable in Phantoam's lair, but on the other hand they had little choice. They did remember Phantoam's invitation for them to go back through any portal-haven they found, and debated this between themselves whenever they got a chance.

The both decided that whatever the next day brought, they would do exactly that, with the first portal-haven they came across.

The Inkwish did not sound like the kind of creatures they

wanted to meet, and although Martin and Dominika had both the key and the inscription to hold on to, they felt Phantoam had given them the most important piece of news, the most important gift so far – that of choice. It made them feel much better that they could leave whenever they wanted to.

As the sun set, Martin realised he would find it difficult to opt out. He did not make any attempt to communicate this to Dominika, who might still be feeling a little unsure, but something inside of him made him realise the weight and importance of his own personal mission.

He had come to some cross-road and his destiny lay ahead. He realised now he would find it very difficult to turn back.

The air grew cooler, but no less stifling with the stench of Phantoam's belching body smell, and they huddled against the far wall, as far from him as possible, just where a passage offered them a slice of fresh air.

Later that evening, Phantoam himself rested his head on the ground, and they themselves felt quite drowsy.

Soon they were all asleep.

But just as each step of the way so far had up to now offered something surprising, not even their wild imagination could have conjured up the unusual creature that would suddenly appear the next morning to escort them to the most important person in Tantalis.

They had come a long way already, but had even further to go.

::: seven :::
Queen Fara

vivat regina
long live the queen

When they woke the early morning light was quite different and what Martin saw directly in front of them so surprised him that he was instantly wide awake. This was not normal for Martin because he was usually a slow riser in the mornings.

The floor of the cave directly under Phantoam, who was now also awake, looked as though it was made of pure gold.

"Ahh. Glad you're with us," said Phantoam, himself a little sleepy still. "I have a journey to make today, so you two will be off to meet someone." He paused, peering above them, and down the passage to the outside of the cave. "I hope she isn't late. Wait a minute, I think I hear someone."

Into the cave and down the opening flew a creature, some seven hundred and fifty millimetres tall. It was neither grotesque-looking, like Trollip, nor particularly beautiful. In some strange way the figure was familiar. It was clearly a female: a human-like body and with wings.

"There you are," said Phantoam obviously relieved. "Glad to see you." He turned his head towards them. "Martin,

Dominika, this is Jezze-B, one of our faery guides and an important assistant. Probably the best tracker in the kingdom and a trusted member of the court. She'll be taking you further." He moved his head towards the faery, nodded and said: "I'll be seeing you again, I am sure."

Jezze-b was still airborne, and flicked her head this way and that, smiling a little at the enormous creature in front of her. She clearly knew him well as she was not intimidated in the least. In fact they seemed to have some understanding.

She then turned to look at Martin and Dominika. It was not a look of appreciation or even one of acknowledgement. In fact had they held her stare they might have realised that it was partially a look of mild contempt.

It was clearly the end of one episode – they were moving on, but where to, they wondered. Martin had so many questions; they had only just had time to get used to Phantoam and now they were leaving. Thoughts of turning back crept into their minds; and one look between them made them realise there was no going back, at least not now.

They said goodbye to Phantaom who seemed to be readying himself to exit the cave, and followed Jezze-B out of his lair.

What they had failed to do the previous day or, perhaps, simply been too afraid to do – stand at the entrance to look out over the vast expanse – they found themselves doing now.

It was a view that took their breath away. Had there been any residue of sleep remaining it was instantly swept aside as they looked down on another forest and a number of green hills in the distance. The hills themselves shimmered from the vibration of their brilliant hue.

Further and beyond, they could just make out a small mountain and a row of trees marching up its side. The look from Jezze-B made them understand this was where they were going.

"So you're a faery," said Dominika.

"So what's it to you ...?" was the reply. This made both Martin and Dominika raise their eyebrows instantly: here was trouble, they thought.

This was no ordinary faery. Certainly not the traditional kind one found in countless books back home. Perhaps simply a disgruntled one on a bad day.

"Of course I am a traditional faery – you're just reading the wrong books," she said adamantly. "And yes, I *do* know what you're thinking most of the time, especially when you're thinking it of *me*. Now let's get going." She flicked her diminutive head in the direction of some stone steps that led them down from Phantoam's high lair onto the forest floor below.

Soon they came to a stream and Jezze-B motioned for

them to clean their faces. They had forgotten about the slimy mud Trollip had made them smear themselves with the previous night. They drank deeply too, the water tasting of mountain reeds, herbs and stones bubbling in the rush of a stream. Soon their stomachs bulged from their fill and when they stood up, they wondered if they would be able to travel any further.

"You don't fly?" said Jezze-B; it was both a statement of mild contempt and a question.

They both shook their heads at one another.

"Phhhiss," she uttered dismissing them with a flick of her wings. "That means we walk."

Martin and Dominika decided to remain silent, not wanting to incite the disgruntled faery into any more insults or impatient comments. But it wasn't long before Dominika walked much closer, up behind Martin and shocked him by saying: "I want to go back at the soonest possible opportunity. I just don't want to go too far into anything without going home first…okay?"

"Okay," he said, thinking that if the portal-havens Trollip spoke about worked it might be a good idea. But how long before they found one and where were they going? He clutched the key again, hoping it would give him some courage and was about to open his mouth to say something to Jezze-B, but decided against it.

It didn't take long though.

"You're not thinking of turning around, are you?" asked Jezze-B. She rose up into the air, her wings fluttering violently, which startled them both. And then she seemed to calm down and ordered them to sit down. From behind a bush she retrieved a pipe which she lit by simply passing her flat hand over the bowl itself. Martin and Dominika stared in disbelief; this *was* a strange faery – perhaps a naughty one as well as a disgruntled one. She puffed gently. "Gives new meaning to feary lights, doesn't it?" she said after blowing a small ring of smoke from her petite, circled lips. She giggled uncontrollably. So much so that Martin wondered if she would begin choking. They both found themselves smiling also.

"Look, I have a job to do; I know I'm not in a very good mood, but the truth of it is that I dislike humans; they bore me, have caused relentless trouble, and quite frankly it's very difficult to feel sympathy for creatures who don't even believe in me. Okay?" She looked at them with an expression that told them that she, herself, was seeking a little sympathy. "We have quite a way to go. You're safe with me as long as we keep on the edge of the forest. Acktare is always above, and that means that any danger is warded off automatically. I am taking you somewhere you will not only enjoy, but to someone who will explain fully what you have to do, why you're here and where you'll be going. You want to go back home? That's fine; of course you can, but not before I've done my job."

She sniffed, wiped her nose with the back of her small hand and looked at them quizzically, seeking some form of recognition and agreement. Martin looked at Dominika, and they both nodded their heads.

"Okay, now keep as silent as possible; if you want to speak, do so in a loud whisper; but no sudden moves, no shouting. See that row of trees? It's the entrance to the palace. It's cool, there's good food, and as much rest as you might need. And what's more you can go home from there, just as you wish." Her large eyes probed them; it was only now they could see their soft pink, salmon colour. In fact they complemented her skin tone so well that, in the morning light, Martin decided she looked quite beautiful.

The forest was similar to the Dark Woods; perhaps an extension – the shapes and textures now came to life. Trees on their left towered above them, the bark unlike the prolific oak trees they were both used to, but instead smooth, with tiny knobs and textured growths all the way up. The leaves, instead of being large in their need to capture limited sunlight, were small, dainty and prolific, showing clearly that sunlight itself was in abundance. Here and there flowers sprouted; a red one, and then suddenly a soft hue of orange or mottled green; again not flowers they had ever seen before.

Jezze-B stopped. Under a tree she picked a flower. It was huge; fanning out into the light, blue creases down from its inner body towards the very outer reaches of its curved, flowing petals.

"Eat this; it is juicy, sweet and very good for you," she said, offering it to them before taking a bite.

Tentatively, they placed a small piece in their mouths. It tasted of fig, and as the light, thin petals broke open into their mouths, they realised they would want more. Jezze-B smiled as she watched them. Fortunately for them they found another three or four each, and they sat under a huge tree, eating contentedly.

Martin thought it okay to say something. "Can I ask you a question?"

"Uhuh," said Jezze-B stopping.

"Was that gold in Phantoam's cave?"

"Uhuh."

Martin looked at her, but didn't comment further.

"You've read in books that dragones steal gold and especially jewellery from young maidens," commented Jezze-B.

"I don't know about the maidens, but I've heard about the gold," interjected Dominika.

"Well – it's rubbish," said Jezze-B, scoffing at the idea. And then she continued, after smacking her lips and patting her hands together as though dusting them off, "We bring it to them and line their caves; at least the trolls do. We find it." She looked at them again, as if making sure they understood clearly: "We faeries don't do that kind of work. That's what trolls are for."

"What does Phantoam do with it?" asked Martin.

"He lies on top of it, of course," she said. And then after seeing their blank expression, she continued, impatiently: "Dragones leak a toxic liquid; it would soon eat up the floor of the cave if it were not for the gold. It's a hydrochloric acid." She watched them very closely. "Don't tell me you don't know how they fly!?"

Martin and Dominika shrugged their shoulders.

"Well, well, well; I did know humans were really stupid sometimes, but this is going too far. All those books and so-called legends about dragons, and they don't even know how they fly!" She let out a little shriek of laughter, but caught herself. "Sorry, I suppose I shouldn't make you feel bad; you can't help it, being human. What you need to think about while we finish our journey today, is how on earth such a large creature, with such small wings, can rise into the air and fly. Now that's a challenge for you two. In the meantime, let's get cracking!" She managed a smile.

They must have reached the bottom of the ravine because soon they were climbing. Martin clutched the key again, seeking from it the strength he needed, while Dominika walked behind, enjoying the colours and shapes of each leaf that came her way; they were darker down here.

To the right, as they parted branches and leaves to one side in order to negotiate a small stream, they noticed a bird on a branch. It was the first they had seen.

From now on they were to see more and more birds, of all shapes and sizes. The climb was difficult but not exhausting and as they neared the summit, both Martin and Dominika kept wondering when they would be getting 'there'. At the top they could see nothing at all and where greeted by three trolls – Martin assumed good ones.

Jezze-B spoke only briefly to them in a strange language while Martin strained to gauge whether it was the same Trollip had spoken. The trolls looked much the same, with only the one decidedly taller; they each wore similar clothing to that which Trollip had worn – a thin leather jacket, with thongs – their swords neatly tucked, and almost invisible, behind them. Martin noticed their top pockets bulged and he assumed they were also full of olives. All three stared at the two humans, a look of suspicion, but also interest. Perhaps Trollip had spoken to them. They actually missed him.

Without having seen it, Jezze-B pointed to an opening in the side of the hill's rock-face, in front of them. They ventured through to find that it widened immediately. What was strange was that when Martin looked back, he could see no opening. The ground immediately smelled different; fresh, clean, alive. After just a few strides they were faced with a large tree towering far too high for them to see its top. Dominika recognized it as a portal-haven, and nudged Martin.

They had to negotiate it by walking around; it was a strange sensation because they had no awareness of anything on the other side until they were there.

What they witnessed took their breath away.

White wisps of soft candyfloss cloud swirled, as if to music, everywhere – amongst the trees, up the side of the rock, over the ground. Smaller trees, wild, yet seemingly planted with the sole purpose of being aesthetically pleasing created an awe-inspiring and tantalizing vision all around them. And the trees were simply thick with birds. This was no faery book scene with twittering birds flying over them like some mystical guide or divine blessing – this was an abundance that shook with green and gold, and white. And it shimmered everywhere with life.

Down they walked, stopping far too often – to touch a branch, reach out for some flurry of movement in the brush, feel the texture of thickly covered bark, or just to marvel. And then there it was.

No magical faery castle, Shangri-La or Utopia. Just breathtaking magnificence in pure ingenuity and design. The building rose majestically, taking one's eye up with it, and then across deeper into a small settlement, each structure complimenting one another. So complete and finished that not one single stone seemed out of place.

And this was just their first impression.

Creepers raced across the walls this way and that; dancing in unison, and the soft, gentle pastel orange and earthy colours of the mottled surface blended with them as though they were part of the construction itself.

Water flowed in front of the main building, with wide steps leading into the entrance, and then around, deeper into the settlement. Somewhere in the distance, they could see a figure in a boat.

The entrance was made from stone, marble-like but not something from the world of humans; it seemed almost to change as they walked, the colours and textures guiding perhaps

112

their own mood and perceptions. There were fountains everywhere, ponds, even though they were now inside. Small tables punctuated the interior – this was where a few trolls sat now. There were others for faeries, seemingly busy at work. And yet other resting places for much larger, or taller creatures. One had a sense immediately that everyone lived here in harmony.

Every now and then they saw great paintings on the walls; scenes, islands, landscapes – most with strange beings in them.

Jezze-B stopped at a beautiful fountain; fish lazed in the pond below, the water jet rising from one side between two carved wings, and aimed so that they could simply position their mouths for a drink, which they did.

They were shown into a courtyard to one side, and sat down on a large bench made from stone. When they did, it dipped like a cushion, around their legs and buttocks, making them relax completely. It was a strange, but welcome sensation.

"Cool bench," said Dominika. "We should have one of these at the bottom of the garden." Martin smiled and touched her on her arm, showing solidarity. He looked around, drinking in as much detail and beauty as he could. Jezze-B raised her right hand slightly, and flew away. They were alone, but not for long.

Across the courtyard with the sun above them, yet not without the wispy light of cloud still evident, walked a figure.

113

Graceful, tall, becoming more and more majestic as she came nearer.

"I didn't want you to be disturbed by my sudden appearance," she said, "I am Queen Fara. I am happy for you to call me just Fara."

She wore a soft satin cloak, and from her head fell the whitest hair they had ever seen; straight as an arrow, and as fine as a spider's web; it disappeared when caught against the wispy white cloud swirling behind her. It was as though the light, the cloud and her body were all in some ritual dance. Martin found it quite impossible to keep his eyes off her.

"Hello," said Martin, very softly and slowly. Dominika said nothing, but simply stared.

Queen Fara sat down on another smaller bench to their right.

"You have come a long way." She smiled, revealing an aspect to her mouth that was enticing and which managed to ignite something deep inside Martin as he looked at her. If ever he had wondered what awakening romance could evoke, he now knew what it was and how it happened. He was unable to say anything again for some time.

Her hair touched the ground now, dislodging itself ever so slightly at her temples, so they could see her perfectly pointed ears, long, thin, and as light as the clouds that floated all around them.

"Welcome to Tantalis," she said, still smiling. Her voice was the kind that could launch a thousand sailors on a never-ending voyage without ever the thought of mutiny. Martin was transfixed.

Queen Fara looked sideways, and then got up, beckoning both of them to follow her. She walked deeper into her court-yard, and stopped at a stone pool; water flowed gently into it along another stone course from somewhere beyond. She pointed to a flower. It had a long stalk and the most beautiful stamen and petals, in blue and purple, with tiny orange flecks inside.

It was moving.

At first Martin and Dominika simply assumed a breeze was blowing. But there was no wind. Then they saw it. An insect, not like any they had ever seen. It was large, black, with the same orange flecks on its back, and looking something like a cross be-tween a beetle and a wasp. It flew around the flower.

But this was no random flight. The two were in perfect unison. This was a dance.

"If you listen really carefully," said Queen Fara, "and close your eyes, you can actually hear the music." They could not close their eyes right now; the scene was too fascinating. The choreographed movements seemed almost perfect; not a single one out of place; each time the insect moved one way the flower did the same, seemingly enticing it, luring it, in a stance and attitude of invitation.

"The flower wants the wasp to deposit his sperm inside her," said Queen Fara, eventually, "she has already assumed a male role and danced with the female wasp, allowing her to deposit her eggs. For her role to be complete, she has had to attract this male wasp who will now deposit his sperm inside her to fertilize the eggs inside."

"Why, why would she want them to do that?" asked Dominika, aghast.

"There is a way of the Circle here in Tantalis, and in all the world before. There is nothing that exists by itself. They have a relationship these two, or three. The flower performs perfect fertilization, and the rearing of baby wasps, even secreting food until they are fully grown, but she receives payment also."

"Payment? Like in money?" asked Martin softly.

Queen Fara smiled, "yes, the currency is the eggs themselves. The parent wasps need only ten or twenty to be hatched, but as many as a thousand eggs are fertilized, giving the plant food and nourishment. I am sorry you weren't here earlier yesterday to see the flower dance with the female wasp. It was quite different; the dance of a supporting male, far less aggressive than now, allowing the female to adopt a more feminine, and graceful stance. Now, she is the female, dancing with the male wasp."

They both stared in amazement. She started walking.

"Believe it or not, there are many examples, although not quite as intricate, of this kind of relationship where you come from, but humans have all but forgotten their place alongside creation. They seem to act alone, don't they?" She looked at them, and for the first time they were able to detect a note of sadness. "Come," she said to them, "I know you want to swim and clean yourselves."

She led them into another courtyard. Three elfin girls stood against the wall, all with instruments in their hands; they were also beautiful, but nothing like the queen. "This is Sharmâ, Kyla and Edytya," said Queen Fara, smiling, "Martin and Dominika; the ones we have been waiting for." The three girls rose, and made a strange sign, turning their left hands gently this way and that and then allowing their palms to drop and face the ground; it was a greeting, they decided. Martin waved shyly back at them.

Near them was a baby tricorn, eating the leaves from a bush that grew up against a high wall; its three tiny horns, the longest nearest to its temple, bobbed as it munched. It was almost entirely white, with a faint hue of pink. It looked up at them and nodded its head, as though in greeting.

"That's Emmazelle; she is a tricorn – things have changed a little since humans were here," said Queen Fara, smiling.

The pool or bath was made of richly coloured stone or slate, in triangular tiles; it looked like a Roman bath, thought Martin, having viewed so many in pictures and models, both in the library and at home with his father. Water entered the pool from a multitude of sources, but the jets that hit the water did so not with a great rush and noise but gently, and with a soft shhhh. There was also a rivulet that ran down a pebbled water-course, meandering as though coming from somewhere precipitous, and ending here. It was the kind of pool anyone could play in all day, exploring each corner, each flow of water, pool, rock formation and floral growth that seem to accompany the overall music of the feature as a whole.

They swam naked, realising only much later that they had taken all their clothes off, yet not feeling embarrassed at all. Neither of them had done this since childhood; it was a strange sensation, and as though everyone could detect their thoughts, a small group of faeries entered, tucked their wings tightly behind their backs and, also without clothing, joined them.

118

Soon everyone was laughing and playing together; Martin aiming some of the jets to catch a faery on her head, while she would disappear under the water and miraculously surface on the other side of him, making the water foam and rise in distinct shapes of various creatures, simply with the flick of her two hands. When Martin turned around to avoid a splashing in his face, he was suddenly confronted with two wide nostrils and three horns. He backed off quickly, a little afraid. But a faery saw him, and jumped up onto Emmazelle's back to show that she was tame. She wandered up and down between the jets of water, stopping every now and then to wet the faery or shiver her shiny coat under the cool spray. And all the time the three elfin girls played their beautiful music.

It was, Martin instinctively realised suddenly, the music of the flower.

It must have been at least two hours before they were quite exhausted and got out to lie on large woollen sheets, drying them instantly, somehow making them feel calm and rejuvenated at the same time.

They dressed and then sat at a low table, their legs crossed on large, billowy cushions, and ate a large assortment of strange fruit and succulently roasted meats. Martin recognised one as the delicious Phisteriss water-rat Phantoam had given them.

"Are we going to see Phantoam again?" asked Dominika.

"Oh, yes," said Queen Fara eyeing them from across the large table. Dominika had not looked at her, but instead was engrossed in the ornate carvings of the many scenes from, she surmised, around Tantalis – those of dragones and faeries, elves, trolls and others. She shook her head when she imagined, no, *saw* some of the figures move. She tried to point this out to Martin, without being noticed.

Queen Fara smiled. "Yes, of course – he's one of my most important advisors, and a good friend." She finished a mouthful of food, and still looking at Dominika, said: "We were not sure if you would come, Dominika, but we're glad you're here now. Have you enjoyed what you've seen so far?"

Dominika looked sideways at Martin, and then uncharacteristically, in a shy tone, replied that she had.

"We weren't sure whom you would tell, Martin. We were a little worried you would tell your mother about the box and key, and that she would discourage you from investigating. In fact I sent Trollip through the portal-haven into your tree at home to meet you one night; but it was Dominika's encouragement that got you both here. We're proud of you both."

They smiled, feeling more comfortable; it was difficult not to be with Queen Fara, but everything was still so strange, and they were not yet quite fully at ease.

"I think it's about time you found out what we expect of you," said Queen Fara, wiping her mouth and hands delicately on a large napkin, also with scenes from Tantalis exquisitely embroidered onto it. Martin raised his eyebrows when he saw her put the napkin down, and a Troll on the table wince, holding his head as though someone had smacked him. She continued:

"Dragones and humans lived in harmony long long ago, teaching us almost everything we know. They taught all ancient kingdoms and societies how to live, and shared secret knowledge with us. Sadly humans became jealous and decided to kill the dragones, one by one, which they began to do. They are particularly vulnerable in their stomachs because of what humans call dragone blood. When pierced with a sharp sword, they secrete this liquid which kills them almost instantly. Many dragones were killed, and we pleaded with humans to stop. We knew it would mean their banishment from Tantalis, or at least the world we all knew back then. I was still a very small child, and remember the awful consequences when the human race was separated from us; we, too, experienced suffering and loss of all kinds, even the loss of some knowledge of the ancient ways itself."

She stopped to take a drink, watching them all the time, and put the large silvery goblet down on the table. This time a

121

faery darted out of the way, so as to miss a direct hit on her own head. From now on both Martin and Dominika lifted their own goblets as often as they dared, placing them down in the middle of a crowd of faeries, or next to a group of sleep trolls, just to see what would happen. It was great fun.

Queen Fara smiled.

"Of course, they did not kill all, but Tantalis withdrew – there was no other course of action left to us – and humans were cut off from the world they now call myth. Today, sadly, the majority follow a path of materialism, forgetting their own spirituality, and not only forgetting us, their original friends and helpers, but also ridiculing, mocking and discouraging belief in us. They live with deep desire for the future, and also with immense pain and trauma of the past. Humans have all but forgotten to live in the Now."

Dominika looked uneasy at this point.

Queen Fara continued: "About the same time, seeing the immense power humans had gained, not only in knowledge but also in warfare, revenge and the death of dragones, a band of elves turned against us. Over some time, as they grew more and more envious of power, more and more covetous of human's success and control of their world, their features changed entirely, and today they are unrecognisable as elves, but we know

122

them as…"

"… the Inkwish," said Martin suddenly.

"You are beginning to grasp the terrible truth," said the Queen, no longer looking at them, but down at the ground, feeling herself both sad and full of regret. For just a fleeting moment, she lost the Presence of Now and entered the past; it washed over her like a cold wind, so that she shivered slightly. When Martin and Dominika looked down at the table, they witnessed all the figures in the various scenes do much the same, some even hiding away furtively behind trees, or plates, or goblets. There was no doubt they, too, were following the story.

Two of the musical faeries, Kyla and Edytya, came forward and repositioned Queen Fara's immensely long hair, neatly onto the ground around her. Fara stopped to thank them; then she continued:

"There is actually a direct link between the Inkwish and humans themselves, without humans realising it. In essence," and she stopped, seemingly to take a deep breath, "the Inkwish have adopted the dark side of human nature; they have become their shadow, not wanting to return to the form or nature of an elf again."

She paused again, regained her composure and thinking deeply said: "Except one …" And then, as if she had second thoughts, continued quickly, "but let's leave that for the time be-ing. Their goal is to influence humans; they cannot take over Tantalis because of us and the dragones, but they realise they can adopt the Earth; conquer it, so to speak, dominate, crush and destroy it.

This they are doing through people now living on Earth, teaching them artful ways to invent chemicals and materials that benefit humans, but which also destroy the planet. If they suc-ceed it means the end of humankind, the Earth itself as we know it and, of course, of us here. So you can see how clever they are."

"I don't understand," said Martin, "why do you not simply kill them all?"

Queen Fara, for the first time, looked almost uncertain of herself. "Well, a simple war; perhaps. Eradication of all Inkwish? Yes; it sounds easy. But …" She paused again, this time reposi-tioning herself on her immense cushion. "You must realise, not only do they embody the dark nature of humankind, the Inkwish are also our dark side, too. It would be like a human killing him-self because he knows he has bad habits, or a cruel nature, or evil intent. One does not naturally kill oneself. It is not something we as elves are proud of and like to talk about openly. We hold the Inkwish at bay; and have greater positive powers over them, in a place where good still triumphs over evil."

But can we ever be sure that killing them off, and therefore killing a part of ourselves, will solve the problem? We don't know. It's that uncertainty that stops us from war; besides although elves are artful in the practice of warfare, it is not something we chose. Death is the supreme enemy of our culture, not in any way an end."

Martin let out a lung-full of hot air pursed through his lips, while trying to digest all this fascinating and serious information.

Just then Magnus burst into the courtyard. Martin and Dominika were delighted to see him, and he gave them both a slobbery kiss before settling down. Martin wanted to ask where he had been, but before he could do so, Queen Fara spoke again:

"I think it's probably about time you returned; you might be just a little tired when you get back, but at least you can sleep late tomorrow." She then paused, looked at Dominika and said with a smile, "we will be seeing you again."

With that she rose, held her two hands on either side of her cheeks in a slow and gentle greeting and disappeared amongst the foliage and water, deep into what lay beyond within her palace.

Edytya beckoned to both Martin and Dominika to follow her, and with Magnus in tow, they moved beyond the courtyard, into a small room on the one side.

"You don't need your key here," she said to Martin. Just place your hand over this portal device, together."

It was a round, smooth metal handle, decorated with a script of some kind, and on top of a short wooden pillar in the middle of the room.

They did as they were told, with Magnus beside them.

The last thing they could remember, was Edytya smiling at them knowingly, but also with a look of encouragement.

When Martin woke, he was in bed. It was something to six, he noticed on his laptop next to him. His eyes were heavy with sleep, and his shoulders were a little chilled. He pulled the blankets over them and shivered with the delight of new-found warmth. He let out a deep sigh, as some of the memories of Tantalis came flooding into his mind. It was too early, he decided, to entertain any thoughts of his recent adventure, and he let them dissipate into that special place between being awake and being asleep.

He fell back against his pillow, vaguely sensing the sheer immovability of his legs stretched out in front of him, and did not wake again until more than two hours later.

As he fell back into a deep sleep, he remembered they would have to retrieve his chair from the bottom of the garden.

If he had known what was waiting for him in the week to

come, he might perhaps have wished he had not returned home at all.

::: nine :::

A Lonely Walk

vox clamantis in deserto
a voice crying in the wilderness

Martin woke to find his chair beside his bed. Dominika must have returned it. There was no sound from the house, only that of Magnus scratching at his door.

He called out. There was no answer, just Magnus.

The house was quite empty, he discovered, except for a note on the kitchen table from his mother: *gone shopping, will bring back treats, love Mom.* Martin went about his morning routine of preparing himself for a new day.

He telephoned Dominika, but there was no one there. And then he realised it was Saturday morning. He retrieved the sleeping bag with a long stick, from the top of the cupboard, replaced the key deep inside it and wrapped it up again. Perhaps he was still a little tired, but it took three throws to get the bag lodged back inside the cupboard.

The weekend dragged on, with Martin flitting back and forth between the reality of his life at home, and that of Tantalis. He spoke only briefly to Dominika on Saturday evening; she too sounded tired, and also not eager to say much. She was leaving with her father to visit her aunt for the night. He missed her, and hoped he would see her at school on Monday and arrange for them to get together.

There was enough homework to keep him busy all of Sunday, but as he worked, he found himself sketching dragones and elves. What was remarkable was the accuracy of his sketches – he had never been particularly good at drawing, and they surprised him.

When his mother entered his room, he was careful to hide them each time.

But he was not as successful at school.

Bleaney Davinporte was the largest and cruellest bully imaginable; and he happened to be in Martin's class. The only triumph Martin had managed over the year was to be able, from his wheelchair, to throw the javelin further than Bleaney. This had not put the bully in a good mood, and when the teacher's back was turned he had mumbled something about a cripple. At first Martin had been hurt, but his success on the field had become well known, not least of all in the paraplegic races held at Robbensfield Preparatory itself, with contestants from all over the country.

The headmaster, Mr Spoke, was particularly proud of the fact that his 'normal' school could accommodate 'all types' and that it had been chosen for such events that year. Martin had become a legend, and his speed in his wheelchair had already won him three cups and four Certificates of Merit in sprinting. The cups were proudly displayed in the foyer with newspaper clippings from The Robbensfield, and apart from Bleaney, all his schoolmates greeted Martin each day with respect, many with a little envy.

But today Davinporte was in the wrong place at the wrong time. So was Martin.

They had just finished pasting in notes and doing drawings of creatures around the world in Environmental Studies, when Davinporte looked over Martin's shoulder.

"What's that. Not another dragon!" he said really loudly. And then he said more quietly: "I've seen you, Martin Fields, drawing dragons and funny creatures – you're supposed to be drawing animals."

The headmaster who also happened to teach them this subject was only three desks away.

"That looks interesting," he said moving backwards to take a look. "Dragons?" Martin quickly hid the drawing.

"He's always doing that, drawing stupid creatures," said Davinporte. "He's not supposed to be doing that, is he Mr Spoke?

"That's enough, Davinporte," said Mr Spoke, turning to

Martin again. "As long as you've done what I asked you, Martin…" It was more a tone of enquiry than anything else.

"Yes, Mr Spoke, I have finished; I was just fooling around."

"That's not true, Mr Spoke, I've been watching him. He's got some of goblins and other stuff also!"

"Alright Davinporte; that'll do, thank you …"

Mr Spoke moved away, giving Martin a chance to take a deep breath of relief. Martin glared at Davinporte and made a face. Davinporte wagged a finger at him, "I'm watching you, Fields."

"Oh, go stick your nose in a donut!" said Martin, contemptuously.

Davinporte lunged forward to grab hold of Martin's wheelchair, his cheeks bulging with effort, but Mr Spoke turned around to address the whole class about a new assignment just in time.

The bell rang. Thank goodness, thought Martin. Everyone exited quickly, leaving him to negotiate the desks and the door alone. Martin did this as quickly as he could before Mr Spoke could say anything.

But Martin would have little relief the rest of the week. He made a point of seeking out Dominika, and for the first day or two she all but avoided him. She smiled when she passed him in

131

the corridor, and told him briefly about her weekend, but that was it.

"We must get together," said Martin, making a face to emphasize a sense of urgency.

"I know, I know, but I'm kind of busy with projects and stuff." She seemed to hesitate. "We can get together on Friday night if you like," she suggested.

"Yes," said Martin, "we've got to go back, Dominika; we've simply *got* to. You know that; and it must be soon, real soon. I just know that Queen Fara needs us to do something really important."

"I'll come around on Friday night for supper. I'll tell my Dad I'm sleeping over, and we can wait for Mara to go to bed like last time. Alright?"

Martin nodded.

"Okay, now I've got to go." She touched the side of his chair and ran off.

Friday did not come too soon. Martin had mulled over each minute of their time in Tantalis, thinking of each conversation, of Trollip, Jezze-B, Phantoam and Queen Fara herself, and everything they had said.

But Friday was not to be a good day at all. In fact, Martin would remember it as one of the most least favourite days of his

132

life.

At lunch, as he wheeled his chair down the long corridor to the cafeteria at the other end, wondering whether he felt like anything to eat at all, he noticed a crowd gathered around the notice board. Must be something important, he thought, as he spun the wheels of his chair faster to catch up with them and see what it was that everyone was looking at.

When he got there he wished he hadn't. There up on the board were at least four of his drawings, one of Phantoam, his name prominently underneath. Another of Trollip, and even one of Queen Fara.

Davinporte was standing in front to one side.

"Come, gather around!" he said, "this is what your hero Martin Fields spends his time doing in class. He actually believes in fairies! Perhaps he's also a fairy..."

Some of his class mates were laughing. But it wasn't their laughter that made him feel as though more than just his legs were paralysed.

It was that Dominika was right in front with her friends. And the fact that she, too, was laughing.

Martin wheeled himself back down the corridor; now he knew he didn't feel like anything to eat.

On Friday afternoon, he spent time after school in his

room preparing himself. He retrieved the key and positioned it up against the wall behind his small fish tank. Now that he knew what to expect, he scoured his cupboard, taking out a number of different sweaters, long pants and jerseys, not able to decide which to wear.

He couldn't make up his mind whether he should have on a t-shirt and sweater or just a sweater and jersey. The pants were easy – he chose long ones with pockets on the side; they were dark blue and not easily visible at night. But his top – he just couldn't decide. He telephoned Dominika to see what she thought, but put the phone down before anyone answered.

"Going on a trip, are we?" asked Mrs Fields. Martin spun around in his chair. He hadn't heard her come in.

"No, no – just taking stock; thought I might need to buy something. Will you take me shopping tomorrow, Mom?"

"Bit tight this month, Master Fields, but tell me what you need and we can see what we can do; there's a new discount store at the mall. By the way, is Dom coming for supper?"

Martin had to think. "She said she was coming but she might have something on this evening; I just can't remember. But she is sleeping over."

"Perhaps it's just the two of us; I've got another favourite – tomato stew with lamb knuckles," she said with a smile, retreating into the passage. "Don't forget to feed your fish – they've been looking a bit hungry lately."

Martin wondered how hungry fish looked. "Okay, Mom," he said with a sigh, and turned back to his bed, checking each item. Another problem was that he had no idea how long he would be gone for this time. Would he have to take a change of underclothing, he wondered. He tucked a clean pair of underpants into the side pocket of his trousers and stuck the velcro strip down securely. Oh, yes, he thought, and a hanky.

Martin licked his lips to show his mother his appreciation and they both finished up in the kitchen, with Martin drying the dishes as he listened to his mother's chatter about a new food product her company was bringing out.

Usually at this time of the week he was really tired, and sitting in front of the television often put him to sleep, but when he wheeled himself away from its glare and down the passage, his mother noticed that he was particularly wide awake.

"I think I'll go to bed and read," he said.

She smiled and waved briefly at him before returning to watch her favourite programme on BBC Prime.

Martin knew she would be engrossed and so, quietly but quickly, he dressed himself and got into bed.

About an hour later, he made sure his light was off, and

pretended to be asleep when his mother popped in to give him a kiss goodnight. He didn't move.

He lay, wide awake, waiting for a sound: a door, the scratch of a key, a shuffle of footsteps on the wooden floor of the passage, and then he realised he had made a mistake by not phoning Dominika again. He couldn't do so now, because an extension was right beside his mother's bed, and it was probably too late; besides he had never before worried about Dominika arriving later on any given evening. He couldn't risk anything to arouse suspicion.

He lay awake for another hour and then positioned himself in his wheelchair; he reached behind the fish tank to retrieve the key and placed it firmly inside the large side-pocket of his trousers.

The passage was dark. His mother's light was out.

As deftly and quietly as he could he wheeled himself out through the sitting room door, to the veranda, and then onto the lawn below.

The battle to get to the path began, and this took him some time, with him looking back for any suspicious movement or light from the house that would tell him either that Dominika had arrived or that his mother was awake.

There was nothing.

Finally he was at the tree.

Magnus sat next to him, full of expectation. Thank goodness he was not a dog that barked generally; although he was black, with only a white napkin around his neck, both grandparents had been Dalmatians: a breed that was well known for their silence.

Martin did not wear a watch, but estimated it must have been another hour that he waited, Magnus now asleep next to him, waking only now and then to raise his ears and peer up against the side of the tree itself.

Martin shook his head sadly. It was now clear to him; Dominika had obviously made up her mind not to come back.

He felt betrayed; devastated in fact. He tried to focus on the tree, and picture his father in front of him on the bench; an image, quite clear, gave him just that little bit of courage he needed.

Holding the key tightly in his left hand, he let go of the armrest of his wheelchair and, slowly and clearly, he repeated the words in the inscription.

This time it was smoother, and instantaneous. In literally a flash they were there. But it was not the portal-haven of last time – the old oak that was in front of them. This time it was quite different. In fact, Martin didn't have the slightest inkling where he was, even after taking a few minutes to look around. What was worse was that this time there was no Trollip to greet him either.

Except for Magnus, Martin was quite alone.

::: ten :::
The Hole

me duce, tuts eris
under my guidance you will be safe

Diablo shifted his great weight from one leg to another.

He was taller than all the other Inkwas; his head at least one quatta (about ten centimetres) above the rest. He glared at the four Inkwas that were digging the hole in front of him, and in a rasping whisper, let out a short explosion of expletives, hurrying them on.

They turned to face him, their tongues flicking in and out nervously and then went back to work immediately.

Diablo's own tongue, large and uncommonly crimson for an Inkwa, flicked too. But his was slow, deliberate, as if each flick, each flutter was the result of a careful calculation of speed and length. It was directed at them. The four workers did not let this fact go unnoticed; any slacking off meant that just one spit, and they would feel the burning of his vile poison on their backs. Like all Inkwish, Diablo had two glands in his throat, each one producing a harmless liquid which, when combined, produced a fiery, toxic chemical that burnt through even thick Inkwish skin.

It was a strange and devilish characteristic of this dark

race: that their own poison could harm few other species; it was poisonous only to themselves. To some, their scars were a brave indication of how they had suffered under vicious leaders. But while they might be seen as a sign of courage, or endurance, it was no fun being on the receiving end of an accurate spit.

And this time Diablo was too close to miss.

He watched closely; the hole he had ordered was to be an exact depth and width – he had something clearly in mind, although those digging had no clue what it was. And he wanted it finished before the first watch began.

An aide slithered in by a side entrance, too afraid to make a sudden move; she had in her hands a Hill snake, still moving hesitantly, and on the very verge of its death throws. She waited patiently until a slight movement of Diablo's head and a recognisable flick of his tongue told her she could approach, which she did. She stopped in front of him, gesticulating some form of greeting and the offering of the creature she held in her hands. Diablo looked at her briefly, nodded and took the snake from her.

He rocked forward, his body coming off his enormous erect tail which otherwise gave him balance, speed in flight, and comfort in sitting, and slumped slightly into the semi-squat position peculiar to Inkwas. With one swift movement, he severed the head and at least a quarter of the snake's body so the remainder quivered, and shook in his hands.

The blood dripped down the corners of his mouth onto his chin, and he irritatingly wiped it off with the back of his small left hand.

He was feeling better already. The aide retreated into semi-darkness, around the side of the cave, while Diablo completed his meal by allowing the remainder of the small but tasty snake to drop into his mouth and down his gaping gullet.

Perhaps he had asked for too much; should he have ordered another two workers, or were four enough, he found himself wondering. Now, his hunger satisfied, he leant forward and peered into the hole; the workers stopped briefly, trying to detect his mood, but decided he was simply in a stance of enquiry, and they continued digging.

Just then two more Inkwas entered. Their entrance was quite different. Not the obsequious and quiet waiting in the wings, like the aide. Theirs was a resolute and more confident presentation. Diablo looked at them both.

"Have you thought about it?"

"Yetthh, Ours," they said obediently, their tongues in unison, flicking out between their lips in an attempt to emulate that of their leader.

141

"It's the only way to go." Armai and Geaddon smiled, but only just noticeably. As the two favourite and trusted soldiers of Diablo's personal guard, they held sway. And they knew it.

The task he had set them, although unprecedented, although quite unique in the history of Tantalis, and one which they had spent only brief moments doubting, was such they would be unable to refuse in the bigger picture of things.

"You have known all your lives the secret of combat," continued Diablo turning fully, to face them. "As long as you catch them unawares, you should have no trouble."

The two nodded.

"You will bring it straight to me in the container ..."

"Yetthh, Ours, we will; there will be no thpilling. No delay."

It was exactly what Diablo wanted to hear and he smiled at them.

"If you do exactly as I say, you will be safe." Diablo belched, but neither of them so much as moved either of their long reptilian eyelids; they were transfixed, quite mesmerised by his sheer confidence and the boldness of his plan.

By the beginning of the first watch the hole was finished. It might have been half a quatta deeper, but Diablo decided it would suffice.

The workers went to their watch relieved, bowing subserviently as they retreated from Diablo's presence. Their leader did not budge, though. In fact he remained next to the hole for some time, peering inside, contemplating, judging, scheming. The expression on his face was one of resolute maliciousness; it was clear he had made up his mind about something, and he was not going to deviate.

Every now and then, as Inkwas do, Diablo leant forward to allow his tail a chance to furl around to the front of his body. His small hands stroked it, and he massaged the taut muscles down its length. Although it could bear his full weight, it was also a sensitive organ, finely tuned and as sharp as a razor at the end. Taking care of one's tail, for an Inkwa, was something akin to the preening of feathers for a bird. It was by far their deadliest weapon; and something told him he would be needing it soon.

Much later that night, and by the end of the second watch Armai and Geaddon returned.

In twenty-one centuries no single act in Tantalis would shake its traditions and its history more than the result of their actions that night. Although the Inkwish had turned and had offered troubled times and dark difficulties for everyone in Tantalis to bear, nothing like this had ever been even contemplated.

Diablo knew it. Although his plans remained quite secret,

he knew that what he had devised would change things forever.

He knew, also, they had succeeded when they handed him the container.

What he didn't know was that Armai and Geaddon had not killed one but two fully grown dragones.

If Diablo had had any remorse and perhaps a little more insight, he might have shivered from the sheer magnitude of this vicious deed. Instead he simply smiled and took the large silver container from them.

In the still of the night, one could hear a faint, almost gentle, shrill-like hiss which signified the start of the third watch.

::: eleven :::

The Great Hall

patris est filius
like father, like son

Edytya had found them after a few disquieting minutes during which Martin had walked around a room filled with armour. It was not a room he had seen before and not the room she had taken them to in order to return home.

This was a cold, almost sterile and unfriendly room and one which Martin was sure had not been entered for a very long time.

Queen Fara was mildly alarmed when Edytya and Martin told her.

"It's strange," she said, sitting down, "I don't think an elf has entered that room, except perhaps to take stock, for at least a few hundred years. There has been no need to; it contains weapons – something we do not use."

"But Trollip carries a sword," said Martin, remembering.

"Yes…" said Queen Fara, deep in thought. "He does, but it's mostly for show; the trolls take pride in their position as engineers and helpers; they see themselves as protectors also. And of course they kill to eat, which we don't." She moved closer to the table Martin now knew quite well, and watched him stare once again at the creatures carved onto its surface. "You miss Dominika, don't you?"

He nodded sadly.

"We are sad too; she is a brave human, perhaps she is just going through a difficult time," said Queen Fara sympathetically.

"I'm finding this difficult also; I think it will be a good thing to keep busy. I can sleep late again tomorrow, so I don't mind if I get tired. What do you want me to do?" asked Martin.

"We have a special gathering in the Great Hall. I need to introduce you to everyone, and we have to make plans to get you to Dragone's Lair."

"You mean Phantoam?" said Martin.

"No, not Phantoam. Your key opens the Box – you remember the one you found buried? The Box here in Tantalis contains the Essence of Dragone, the original dragone from the beginning of time. His Essence flooded the known world when we lived with humans and we were able to live in peace. We held the key given to us by him but never really knew why or how to use it, until the Inkwish turned. Since then, we have been trying to find a way to open the box and restore the precious balance."

"I understand that; but why haven't you simply done so – you've waited all this time?" said Martin.

"There was no way for any of us to do it; we simply held the key in safekeeping. We have been waiting for centuries, aeons for an Inkwa to turn to their former self. The key will fit only if a rehabilitated Inkwa uses it."

Queen Fara paused to take a drink, and Martin watched eagerly for her to put her goblet down on the table, hoping he might see a faery or troll having to scurry out of the way. She placed it down on some open ground, and Martin could detect only the flattening of a field of grass next to a tree as she did so.

"It is complicated, but you will have to see for yourself in the Great Hall. Things will become clear to you there – why you're here and what your purpose is. Come, walk with me." Magnus rose and followed her immediately.

The three musicians Edytya, Kyla and Sharmâ walked behind them both as Queen Fara made her way, lowering her head to avoid the overhang of a large fern. She stopped at the flower they had discovered on the previous visit. "See, you've only been gone a short while, but already the tiny wasps are growing inside her."

Martin peered inside and marvelled at the tiny creatures moving around, secure within their own nursery. They walked deeper into the courtyard, past streams of water and plants that almost crowded them; it must be like walking in a tropical forest,

147

thought Martin, although he had never done so. There was so much to see, but he dared not stop. He made sure he never left Queen Fara's side.

The Great Hall was frightening in its size and magnificence. It took Martin's breath away as they entered, and he faltered at the entrance, allowing Edytya to take hold of his arm. Instinctively he fumbled for the key, and took a deep breath.

Columns rose to a ceiling so far above that Martin simply could not tell how high, or where they ended. Strong beams of light streamed in under the ceiling – there must have been an enormous opening at the top, on the sides. He lowered his head, dizzy, his eyes hurting from the effort, and the glare.

The columns had the texture of marble but felt more like wood to the touch; their appearance was mottled, with a myriad of browns, deep reds and orange hues ornately patterned. They were so beautiful that he could imagine himself mesmerised, unable to focus on anything else if he continued staring.

The expanse of the hall itself was beyond his ability to comprehend – it must have been easily the size of three or four soccer fields.

"This is where we meet." Queen Fara walked towards the centre. As she did so, Martin realised that what he had imagined to be an empty hall, was nothing of the sort. There must have

148

been at least one hundred creatures in a large circle, and in the centre, a stone structure. Queen Fara moved back to a chair in the circle, not unlike a throne; the two side supports rose three or four metres into the air, and were carved all the way to the top. There was another chair next to her and she beckoned for Martin to sit in it. He did so.

She paused, and then nodded, issuing to everyone what seemed to Martin like a greeting in Elfin. Only then did Martin realise how the size of the Great Hall and his eyes had deceived him. The throng of creatures – trolls, faeries and elves moved, shifting themselves on their feet, in reverence to their queen. There were many more than he had originally thought.

Just then a faery walked up to Queen Fara and whispered something in her ear. She looked up. When Martin followed her gaze, what he saw made him gawk. Right at the top, and against the thick sharp light, was the tiny silhouette of a dragone.

It did not remain small, though. Silently at first, and then with a gentle, but clear explosion that was a little familiar, it descended, growing larger and larger. Martin almost ducked, wondering where it would finally land.

But there was no need. When the dragone finally came to rest, not only was it almost entirely silent (there was no frantic flapping of its wings, as one might have expected), but it rested

149

squarely on a clearly demarcated area to one side. When Martin looked down at the floor, he realised that this area, too, was covered in gold.

And when he looked up at the dragone, he realised it was Phantoam.

"Please forgive me, Queen Fara," he said, "but I am having a little difficulty with my entry, these days."

There was universal laughter – a laughter of sincere sympathy, not at anyone's expense but a laughter, Martin noticed, that was gentle and made them all relax. Queen Fara smiled.

"Morduainè – this is the one we have spoken about." She looked sideways at Martin, who in turn fixed his eyes on her, uncertain what he should be doing. "You can remain there," she said, "but look in front of you."

Martin turned his head. He jumped.

This elf, tall and almost a male version of Fara, had come from nowhere it seemed; but here he was right in front of Martin, smiling at him. "I am very pleased to finally meet you, Martin. Have you seen some wonderful things here in Tantalis?"

"Yes; yes, thank you," said Martin hesitantly. Another elf spoke also, probably only to himself or perhaps the person next to him, as did a troll. And both miraculously, as they spoke, appeared before Martin and then retreated to their positions far away, across the Great Hall. In all this, they had not raised their voices at all, and Martin was able to hear everything they said, clearly. Morduainè spoke again: "We are sure you are the right person; and are honoured to have you with us." And then he turned to address the great assembly:

"Queen Fara has asked me to direct. I greet everyone." There was a general reply from those assembled around the hall.

"We have waited for this human child for a long time, and he is here. We all know of his mission, having lived in expectation of this one event for centuries. Paul of the Bible echoed this when he said, 'We know that the whole of creation has been groaning together until now.'

There can be only one aim; one purpose – the reunification of Tantalis with the world of humans, as before. We know that the Essence left behind by Dragone, remains secure in his lair, never entered, never disturbed." Morduainè raised his arm and pointed to the stone pediment in the middle of the Great Hall.

An image, at first swirling, and then still and clear, rose out of the stone and came to rest about a metre above it. Martin could see it clearly – it was a lair or cave, and deep within it, as the image drew his eye, as would a camera, there up against the far wall was what they called The Box. It was almost exactly like

151

the one his father had given him. He recognised the ornate carvings. It was much larger, though. Morduainè continued:

"We know that for the Presence of Past and Future to be balanced again, the Presence of Now must be released when the box is opened. We expect too that the Inkwish will lose their power and will return to their former state as elves, although not to their former glory; they will be forever not quite as us, but without their guile, without their dark side. We know too that this Presence of Now will also begin slowly to filter back to humankind, through the portals, through those of us who return from time to time. And now, of course, through Martin and those he comes to influence."

Martin half sniggered, although careful not to let anyone notice. He was having second thoughts, wondering how any of *his* efforts could bring about any change back home. Queen Fara had spoken about pollution, greed and the linear thinking of the Western world; how humans had so badly changed things for the worse. Were they actually expecting him to turn things around? He couldn't help thinking of his drawings, and Bleaney Davinporte.

Perhaps this was all a little too much like a fantasy.

"It is clear that one person cannot do much on his own." Morduainè turned to Martin. Oh, no, thought Martin – if Jezze-B could read their thoughts, his must be like clashing cymbals right now.

Martin obviously had a fated connection with the mechanisms of Tantalis because in the image in the centre of the room appeared his drawings, Bleaney Davinporte, and the entire scene, just as he had imagined it. He looked down, blushing horribly.

"Martin, you have come from a great line of humans; understand us well. No person here is expecting you to do anything on your own; it will be the power of the Presence of Now – the Essence itself that will unleash a whirlwind of change across creation. It is only for you to stand and watch. What you have been called to do is deliver the key, to believe, to rise above your doubt and disability – all of which you have done. Both Moses and Churchill stuttered, yet both were chosen to speak for God and for mankind. Even though you cannot walk, your very journey is a walk of great courage. And you have already embarked on it well. You have all of Tantalis behind you and beside you – a gracious queen, her court advisors and friends such as myself and even the faeries, despite their mistrust of humans. And of course the dragones and trusted trolls."

All around him he could feel hands, voices, sighs and words of encouragement, as a great throng of beings reached out to him. If there had been any doubt in his mind, it was now dispelled.

"We are not saying that the path will be easy. But you of all people know that the Godhead does not expect of us that which we are unable to bare." Morduainè paused, allowing all this to sink in, but when Martin looked at him, he realised he wanted to say something.

The assembly was silent.

"I...I am glad that, that you are behind me; I must admit that...that I was a little afraid of what I must do; not that I am absolutely sure what I must do..." Martin felt himself stumbling. "I don't understand why you don't open the Box yourselves...," he said eventually.

There was a hushed silence; perhaps he had said something terrible, perhaps he had uncovered something they were afraid of. He did not know.

Queen Fara looked at him, drawing his attention away from the assembly. Martin leant in his chair towards her; she bent over and touched his arm, squeezed it and then turned back to Morduainè. She nodded.

"Martin," he said, "you will not be opening the box alone. In a sense, your work is almost complete. You have the key and you will soon give it to us. There is only one who can open the box itself and allow the Essence to work." Everyone was silent again.

Martin looked around, with many of the figures so far away they were as tiny as dots; he was hoping someone would come forward and say something – the suspense was killing him.

"It has to be an Inkwa who has turned, back to us. A fully rehabilitated one. The dark nature had to turn and face the light. Just as Christ was fully God and also fully human. He had to turn so that He became embodied with evil on the cross, and only then could he unleash forgiveness for mankind. This Inkwa must do something even stranger than Christ did - turn from elf, to Inkwa, and back again, the circle complete.

So too with the Essence, with the balance humans need right now – only one who has turned can open the box. Not one of us; not any of us. We have not gone there and come back."

"So ..., so who can do this; where will you find this person?" Suddenly a fear gripped Martin. "Are you wanting me to, to become an, ... an Inkwa?" he struggled again, not knowing fully what they were saying or expecting of him.

"Sshh," said Queen Fara, touching him gently on his arm. "No Martin; it cannot be you, but it is a person before you ..." And with that she pointed resolutely to an image in the centre of the Hall.

Martin looked squarely at a giant of a figure. At first he

couldn't make out if it was a large reptile or a large man. Queen Fara continued:

"See an image of an Inkwa; but look carefully, believing all the time that the image will change. It is mostly your belief that will allow the transformation. Don't think of the past or the future, just enter the image in your mind; take your time. There, you go. Look carefully."

Her words trailed off as if in some dream, and Martin found himself entering what was almost a holographic picture that moved in the centre of the Great Hall, yet right in front of him. He tried to relax, taking a deep breath, but the image of the Inkwa was a little frightening – taller than six feet, with small, ornate scales all over its body, it looked like a cross between a lizard, a snake and a human being. At first quite ugly, and then becoming somewhat attractive, and then…

Then it happened – there had been a gradual change at first, but now … no morphing of the images he had so often made in sequential steps on his computer back home – no overlay. Suddenly it was there – the image of a tall man, beautiful and strong.

The man was smiling at Martin.

But Martin found he was shaking, and before he could check himself, the tears rolled down his cheeks.

The great assembly sighed, their collective voice of sympathy rushing forward to comfort him. Quite clearly before him stood the most beautiful image, not of the terrible Inkwa he had seen, but that of a creature changed into a man.

And the man was Martin's father.

::: twelve :::
A Shameful Descent

in tenebris
into darkness

Martin could feel a presence next to him. There was a hand on his arm, and he raised his hand to wipe the tears from his cheeks.

He felt embarrassed to be crying in front of onlookers, but when he turned he realised it was only Trollip, with Magnus wagging his tail beside him.

"You must not cry," said Trollip. "What happened is good; good thing. Only trolls cry because of the great sadness. Come-come, Martin, we must do so many things."

Martin got to his feet and looked at Trollip – he himself was sad, and busy wiping a few tears from his own eyes.

"Where did everyone go?" asked Martin.

"OoOoooo-ee, *home*. Yeees," said Trollip, as though amazed at the question. "But you not go home *now*; you stay here, and see your father and talk with him. I must take you to him. Not dangerous; not bad place because Inkwish never go there. No-place-land. He's there waiting for you, now. Come."

They exited the Great Hall. Just as Martin did so, he looked up and there up against the ceiling was the tiny silhouette of

158

Phantoam, himself exiting through the opening at the top. There was no sound, except for one final, almost inaudible explosion of fire as he reached the open air at the very top.

They walked briskly into the courtyard past the benches and tables, to a throng of faeries waiting for them. What happened next surprised Martin. Jezze-B and a band of faeries were buzzing around, clearly upset about something, interrupting one another; even pushing and pulling one another. Morduainè appeared. His tall figure and shoulder length white hair made him a prominent figure amongst the diminutive faeries and Trollip himself. There was some disagreement between the faery group and Trollip and some trolls, who looked at one stage as though they might even draw their swords. Martin had never witnessed this kind of exchange between groups before; to him it seemed entirely out of place in Tantalis. Occasionally a disagreement, perhaps, and in most cases humour or the intervention from someone else meant it was quickly forgotten. This had been ugly; rude. Neither had anyone before spoken any language other than English in Martin's presence.

Morduainè seemed disturbed by what he could see and shook his head. He turned to Martin.

"There is something wrong; they never disagree as much as this. It seems the faeries consider the journey to your father in what you call no-man's land, to be *their* prerogative. Trollip is adamant that he must take you, as there might be bad trolls along the way."

He paused and stood still for some time, as though sniffing the air. Everyone around him was dutifully silent, not daring to interrupt or continue with their dispute. "I am worried, I must admit. Whatever disharmony we experience here in this place, means a greater one has taken place elsewhere. Perhaps you must not go at all. It might be better to return to the Great Hall and speak with your father through the Console."

He turned to Trollip, "Take Martin back to his father at the Console and leave him there alone ... unless you want Trollip to stay." He turned to Martin.

"I would like to see my father, but ... if I can just talk to him alone please?" Martin didn't want to offend Trollip.

Morduainè nodded. They returned.

Martin looked at Trollip for guidance once they reached the Console. The empty hall, for all its beauty, was disquieting.

"You think of him; you call him."

"Will you wait for me ... over there?" He pointed to Queen Fara's throne in the circle. Trollip nodded.

Martin looked up and thought of his father, and then faltered; he was so eager to speak with him, but at the same time afraid of his own reaction.

A beam of light rose from the Console, flickered and then the image began to form. There was a voice, faint, faltering, broken. Martin had to strain to hear.

"Martin, hello! Think of me, of us. It's okay ..."

His father appeared again. Magnus barked loudly.

"They were going to bring you to me, but perhaps they think it's too dangerous. I can sense danger from here; something is happening in Tantalis. You mustn't be harmed, not now ..."

"Dad ..." Martin felt a tear welling up again, and looked back at Trollip for support. But his father spoke:

"It's okay. You've come this far, and I am proud of you. Soon we can be together again, not as before, of course, but both of us have a great task ahead of us. Do you have the key?"

"Yes, Dad," Martin placed his hand against his trouser leg and clutched it tightly.

"How does it feel to walk again?" His father said after a brief pause. He was smiling.

"It's great!" said Martin, managing a smile himself.

Martin could clearly sense the danger in the air; he felt almost uncomfortable talking now; it was not as before. But he was determined to keep the image of his father in front of him, and besides there was so much to say.

"I can't believe it. You were an Inkwa?"

"Yes; I am the only one to have gone there and come back. In fact I served Diablo, the leader of the Inkwish for some time – of course I can clearly remember it all now." Martin's father hesitated. "You know, Martin, there was always something worrying me when I was with you at home, when I was your father. It was as though I knew I belonged somewhere else."

Martin stared at the image in the console, speechless. His father looked down, but continued:

"Anyway, then I turned. For some reason it is not something I remember easily. All that remains is the excruciating pain I felt inside myself, inside my body and inside my own mind. Sometimes I imagine it must be something akin to being born. The struggle was ... was, painful. I can think of no other word. As I approached my elfin state, it became easier; the last few steps were a pleasure. And, of course, the feeling of being back; back as a full-blown elf. It was just wonderful!" His father paused, smiling.

Martin was smiling too, but he was more in a stupor than anything else, and his smile looked automatic; that of a mimic: his mind was racing, trying desperately to remember, to place his father – once an elf, then an Inkwa, now an elf again. Yet he had

162

to remind himself that although he was talking to 'his father', this was someone else. He suddenly realised his mouth was open and he could feel a drop of saliva dribble down the one side. He quickly closed his mouth and wiped it with the inside of his hand.

His father looked down again.

"I made a foolish error though. I should not have taken the key with me. There was great commotion in Tantalis, and I was afraid that Diablo would get hold of it and destroy or hide it."

Martin battled between tying to understand the events of his past and the current mood in Tantalis which was clearly tense. He shook his head and his fringe fell onto his eyebrows; he brushed it away, slightly irritated.

"I still don't understand about the key and the Box of Essence," said Martin, now suddenly feeling courage run right through him again. "Why did you not simply open the box and have the other Inkwas turn themselves?"

"It is not the magical box some think it is; Inkwas will not automatically turn – they have to make the choice. The Essence from Dragone's Box releases the potential and lifts the dark pressure off all Inkwas. Many, perhaps even all, will turn again, but it is not a certainty. Also you must understand it's not only about rehabilitating Tantalis and dark Inkwas ..."

Martin interrupted: "But they said that once this happens

Tantalis will be reunited with humans and harmony ... or something, will begin," said Martin, now slightly impatient.

"Yes, that is precisely what will happen, but the Circle is complete only when a human is involved. That is also why I went to live with the humans – becoming one allowed me to return to Tantalis as a fully rehabilitated elf, *and* a human. The Circle would have been complete if I had used the key. That is precisely what I planned to do, but the Inkwish killed me before I could return with it and open the Box."

Martin looked down and shook his head. "I wish Dominika was here; she really understands this stuff much better than I do. You say they killed you – that means you returned here without the key. Why didn't I find the key the first time?"

"I have a portal of my own and returned many times – my goal was to lure you, so I played a bit of a game of cat and mouse – I hope you're not too angry with me, Martin?" His father had a way of turning a difficult situation around; the tone of his voice was now suddenly so familiar; with a comical edge to it. It was his old father back again, and Martin found himself laughing. He was feeling much better. Out of the corner of his eye he could see Trollip shift from one leg to the other next to Fara's throne.

"Okay, as Dominika would say, let's see if I get this straight. You were my Dad back home with the key all the time;

the Inkwas killed you because they knew that if you returned to Tantalis as a rehabilitated Inkwa *and* as a human you would use the key to open the Box and that would be the end of them. You came back to fetch the key, but didn't ... I think I'm getting a bit lost again," said Martin.

"You've got the gist of it, son. I am a fully rehabilitated elf again. The first of a kind! What you see is me as your father, of course, because that's how you know me. I can show you my real self if you would like?"

Martin hesitated; there had been enough surprises already, and he had just managed to regain some composure. Now he would have to get used to another form, another person – no, not another person, but another image. He took a deep breath, and nodded.

The image began to change, and the Professor Fields, as Martin knew him slowly became the real person or 'being' that he was now – a tall, majestic Elf. He was remarkably handsome and, yes, thought Martin, even better looking than Morduainè himself.

"You're ... you're quite someone else! That's cool! But I think I prefer you as my Dad, thank you," said Martin; now suddenly more composed, and a little serious. The image changed once more, and his father spoke again.

"You must realise, Martin, that your father – his body, is

165

buried – you were at my funeral. I simply took the form of his body for many years in the human world. That's what Inkwas do unfortunately. And Elves, of course, but less frequently."

"So where are you now? I mean, you were waiting for me to bring the key back. You could have done this yourself, right?"

"Yes, but without a human presence, believing, wanting to be here and with a defined purpose, the full Circle can never be completed. Remember, the goal of Tantalis is to return to its former glory – that of living with human beings in harmony. So me returning just to give the Inkwish a chance to turn was only a part of it."

"Okay I've got it, I think," said Martin sitting down in the Great Hall, "but why haven't the Inkwas captured you?"

"Well, they're not quite sure where I am. Remember this is no-man's-land. Besides what would they do with me? I wasn't a danger to them without the key, only a partial embarrassment. And up until now Inkwas were never really into killing anything, least of all their former selves, the elves. There has been no kill-ing in Tantalis ever, except for the original death of dragones by humans, which disgusted even Inkwas, believe it or not.

But things have changed. I can sense that something has changed in the last few days. Even Morduainè can feel it. Inkwas have made lots of trouble over the centuries, but this is somehow different; perhaps it's the former Inkwa inside of me, but I feel deeply disturbed. I want you to go back to Mom until I call you."

"Why?" asked Martin, his brown eyes suddenly becoming large with surprise. Now that he had found his father and he was talking of missions and tasks, he couldn't believe he had to go back home.

"I think she will want you to tell her what has happened, and because I am not sure what is about to happen.

You must leave the key here. If I sense further danger, I might have to open the Box and start the process myself, even if it means leaving the element of humans out of it – the full turning of the Circle can happen some other time."

Martin thought about this, but wasn't convinced. Hardly ever had he countered his father; but then this wasn't his father talking. Or was it?

"I understand you want to protect me – you say the Ink-was are not that concerned about you, but I am a definite threat to them. That means that my presence is really important, right?"

"Of course," said his Father. "You are vital. Tantalis is not much without the destiny of humans themselves. Without the reunification of the human world, there is not much reason for us being here. The ultimate goal is the reunification of Tantalis with humans – that's why your presence is so much of a threat. The

Inkwas want the world and the world of people for themselves. That's the *real* power. And some of us feel that they will get it, unless Tantalis and Man are united once again." His father paused.

Martin edged forward as though expecting some deep revelation; his resolve to stay was growing, even in the face of the mounting concern his father seemed to be expressing. He simply did not want to go back. His father continued, somewhat softer than before:

"It's not salvation that the key will bring about – God did that for them. It's rather an orientation. A direction. It's a way of being. It's the unification, or re-unification of Tantalis and the human world for our benefit and for theirs. Humans have lost their way; they have abandoned their mythical and mystical side almost entirely. And only Tantalis can bring it back."

"Man! God, faeries, trolls, elves and Inkwas – and I'm right in the middle," said Martin shaking his head.

"But in fact ..." and Martin's father stopped and looked down at him, as he always had done, "you're the final and most important key. Do you see it now? We can get Tantalis back on track and humans themselves reunited with their mythical selves. But this won't happen without the human element present. And that's you!"

Martin was deep in thought.

"Wait a minute – there's something else. Everybody, Trol-lip, even Queen Fara talks about another time ... no, not really another time, but another Tantalis, another place almost. They speak as though Tantalis was something else before; or that it was somewhere else in some other time ..."

"Oh, my," said Professor Fields, just as he might have done back home, "I am so proud of you, Martin Fields. You *have* been listening! Tantalis is just a former shadow of itself, just as the world is just a shadow of what it was and could be! Look care-fully."

Martin saw before his eyes his father disappear and the word T A N T A L I S being changed into something else. He blinked and saw the letters of the word change: the T moved a few places, the A moved a little to the beginning of another word, another T... and then, suddenly, there it was:

A T L A N T I S – the letters were floating, bathed in creamy light, and the very floor of the Great Hall seemed to shudder.

Martin placed both his hands on the floor itself to steady himself. Trollip let out a whoop of delight and surprise. The shudder subsided and there before them both was Martin's father holding the word *Atlantis* in his hands; like some delicate jewel,

169

it hovered right in the middle of his palm.

"Atlantis?! You've got to be kidding!" said Martin. "You mean that's not just a legend?"

"Legend?" said the form and voice of Professor Fields. "Nothing is a legend without some truth beneath the surface, remember?"

Martin burst out laughing – how often had he heard his father say those words? How many artefacts could Martin remember them both holding and his father repeating this saying over and over: *no legend without some truth beneath the surface!*

"Man, that's cool!"

"Oh, cool indeed – this is not about some 'mythical' non-existent place. This is about the once legendary land and community that served mankind for centuries before they were expelled. That's why beings here are so sad, and also so keen to reunite."

In the background, Martin could hear Trollip begin to wail loudly. He turned around and saw that he was on the floor of the Great Hall, holding onto the legs of Queen Fara's throne for support.

But the sweet moment of discovery and revelation was soon over. The was a quick, abrupt intrusion; as though someone had slammed a door in the middle of a quiet interlude: it was like the interruption of a sharp scream, or a rude screech of a loud machine; the swift and loud clang of a sword coming down on stone.

The Great Hall shook. A loud explosion above them made Martin look up. It was Phantoam descending, almost frantic, faltering in his descent, spewing out fire and flame as his gargantuan body buffeted the sides of the descending columns. He was having a very bad time coming down; if anything his descent was far too quick. Magnus drew closer to Martin's side, whimpering softly.

"Damnation! – I am so tired of old age," shouted Phantoam. "Call Morduainè! Call Queen Fara! – All hell itself has been loosened here in Tantalis!"

Wham! He landed with a deafening crash on the floor and not at all in the middle of the circle.

"Aahhh! You cannot imagine what has happened. Is there anyone here? Oh, no!"

He paused to regain his breath. "They have killed. They have killed two dragones – can you imagine?! These terrible evil Inkwas!"

For just a few seconds there was silence. A heaviness descended. It seemed to crush them, as though life itself was being pressed out of the three of them. And then Martin's father spoke.

"Quick," he said to Martin – you must go. Trollip!" He was shouting now. "Take Martin to the quickest portal – he must return immediately."

He looked at Martin, bending down this time to look him straight in the eye: "Go back, tell Mom everything – you must have her support to return. And come back only when I call you, do you hear me?!"

"Yes, father. I understand," said Martin.

"But leave the key with Morduainè; we might have to use it without you, to turn the Inkwish if things get out of hand. Do as I say. Hurry!"

Martin took one last look at his father, but before he could wave or say goodbye, Trollip was at his side and leading him to the exit.

Seconds later they ran out of the Great Hall, leaving a steaming and fuzzy column of light emanating from the Console, and Phantoam lying, as though himself wounded, on the great floor itself.

::: thirteen :::
Four Mistakes

non libet
it does not please me

The courtyard of Queen Fara's palace swarmed with creatures flying this way and that. Beyond the palace itself it was clear the large settlement of elves was preparing for war. Morduainè himself wore an arrow sling on his back and a short-arm combat knife at his side.

"This is not good," he said as he looked at Martin, "I suggest you give me the key. If the Inkwish are killing dragones, they have clearly decided to capture you."

Martin hesitated, his hand firmly on its shaft – he could feel the engraved surface pressing against the side of his leg. "My strength comes from the key; that's how I walk here," he said. "I won't be able to come back."

"No, no," said Morduainè, "you can't imagine it was only the key? It's the key inside of *you*, Martin. The actual key only directed your attention towards the strength itself, towards us, the portal-haven, and the power of the Essence. You will find that going back without it is quite alright. Besides I don't think you should return here until we call you. Didn't Ish-chær say he

173

would call you?"

So *that* was his real name, thought Martin.

He nodded, now smiling. It was good to hear his father's new name.

"Okay – he's your link," said Morduainè. "I do think that's the best. But be watchful on the other side. Don't trust anyone back home; stick to your routine and speak of this to no one. Be suspicious if anyone asks you questions, like *where have you been*, or *do you believe in dragons?* – these could easily be Ink-wish in possession."

Martin took the key out of his pocket. As he gave this one powerful symbol, this one mighty 'weapon' away, he wondered whether he would ever see it again. But he knew he should not entertain such doubts; it would be in the best hands in Tantalis. And if things got really bad, his father would need it, certainly more than he would. He corrected himself: the elf Ish-chær would need it.

Trollip led Martin to the room Edytya had taken them to for their first return. It instantly reminded Martin of Dominika; her hand touching his for support and reassurance. He found himself shaking his head – how she would have loved the Great Hall! He needed her right now to be able to go back with him and wait for his father's call. To talk to.

Life might be full of choices, but it was also sometimes cruel, taking his father away and then giving him back again but this time a father that wasn't his to enjoy back home. And then his best friend, turning against him.

Terrible things had been unleashed; the battle for Atlantis was taking place not only across the landscape of Tantalis, but indeed right within Martin's own life. He came to his senses and realised that he had no choice but to leave; the portal device stood before him, waiting.

Martin shook Trollip's knobbly hand; they had become firm friends by now and Martin actually felt a tinge of sadness at leaving him behind. He hoped he would be safe. Trollip didn't say anything. He nodded, smiling faintly.

Martin placed his hand over the portal device. It was instantaneous.

Back home in his room he marvelled at how smooth the transport had become. Magnus immediately lay down next to his bed between his chair and bookcase and Martin fell back against his pillow, quite exhausted.

Just wait, he thought, till I tell Dominika and Mom what's happened. He wondered if Dominika was free the next day for supper – he would phone her in the morning. He looked at his clock: it was already past midnight.

175

Dark images shook the corners of his mind, making him tremble until he patted the bed and invited Magnus to lie next to him. With his arm around his neck, he finally yielded to his own physical exhaustion and fell into a deep but troubled sleep.

But Martin's plans for drumming up some support the next day would not materialise.

Four mistakes were in the making that night.

Firstly, Ish-chær had all but pinpointed Martin by appearing before him and making plans with him; the heightened awareness of the Inkwish and their resolve to do evil was now indubitably focussed towards evil; it was so finely tuned that images of Martin and those around him, and even some of their intentions were filtering through like faint radio signals. If specific details were not always clear, often their intentions were; and the Inkwish were picking them up.

Once thing was no longer unquestionable: Martin's presence and his mission was clear.

Diablo had already made plans and now was the time to execute them. The hole was complete, its purpose plain. Only one thing remained: its occupant.

There had been a second mistake. This time it was made by someone a little more unexpected. Bleaney Davinporte had himself become mildly obsessed with Martin's drawings. Forever the consummate bully and always seeking to vent his anger on those around him, he lay on his bed at home, scheming his next move at school on Monday.

What would it be, wings for his little crippled friend Martin? A crown of flowers on his head in the English class? He began to laugh.

Little did he know, though, that he was busy himself unleashing a force far darker than even his own darkest thoughts might have been able to imagine. But how could a boy of his age understand that merely toying with darkness itself might indeed set free forces unknown to him?

Yet something deep inside him did know. Any bully knows what they are doing when they set free their manipulative and cruel schemes – here too, Bleaney could sense some others besides faeries and elves in the strange and enticing world Martin had alluded to.

And something made him want to know them.

He tried hard to imagine them – what did they look like? Were they evil? Did they have weapons? Why did they not kill the faeries? He would, he thought. Who wants faeries? He would become one of them; cruel or otherwise. He would entice them into his mind, his room. Perhaps he, too, would be invited to enter Martin's land.

He shivered.

Less than two kilometres away, as any bird would fly, out-side Martin's window there was a movement in the tree.

As the branches parted a creature landed with a soft thud on the ground. But it was only Magnus who, for a brief moment, raised his head and cocked his ear, before falling back to sleep.

Perhaps for practical reasons, perhaps only because of the clear picture of Magnus lying next to Martin, the creature re-treated to the safety of the old oak, there to lie in anticipation of the right moment. There was no question of it entering now; there was one thing it was trained to do, and that was wait. And it would not have to wait very long.

The next day the moment arrived.

Martin's mother busied herself in the kitchen, in and out of the walk-in cold room in which she kept all her creations and experiments. She had been working on a new dish for some weeks, and it was nearing completion. Finally satisfied, she real-ised she needed to leave for work and wouldn't be back until late that afternoon.

She peered into Martin's room and, deciding not to wake him, let Magnus out and then looked around for something to write him a note.

The note laid out plans for the day: she had some lunch

for him in the cold room, Dominika had telephoned and was coming that evening, and she would be back around five. She placed it on his bedside table, sure that he would see it upon waking.

And then the familiar whine of the Renault's engine indicated to anyone listening that she was reversing out of the driveway.

Seldom, if ever, did she leave Martin at home for so long, and seldom did she work over weekends. If she did pause to think about this, it was only for a brief second; then she put the car into gear and drove away.

This was, undoubtedly, mistake number three.

About two hours later, Martin woke; his head thick with dreams, and memories of his time back in Tantalis. He called Magnus, but there was no answer. He must be out walking in the neighbourhood, he decided, having taken a look out of his window. It was late morning his clock told him. Then he found the note.

Personal ablutions followed; within thirty minutes he was washed, ready for the day and a little more spirited, knowing that Dominika would be coming around later. Perhaps she wanted to apologise, he thought to himself. Perhaps she would return with him. At any rate, at least she could give him some support when he told his mother what had happened.

He remembered his father's words: *tell Mom everything.* Suddenly he wasn't so sure about this. His mother would probably freak? Would she, could she even begin to understand? Was it not simply something any father would say automatically: tell Mom? And then he remembered that it had only been the image of his father talking. He began to doubt whether he would ever, could ever tell her.

She would probably refuse to let him go back. What then?

He was suddenly very hungry and decided to wheel himself, as he often did, down the long passage and then finally through the large door of the walk-in cold room. And this time he managed to do this without bashing his fingers against the door frame.

But Martin was deep in thought.

Had he been a little more vigilant he might have noticed something strange in the house. To his right, as he wheeled himself across the entrance hall and left into the kitchen, he might have noticed the front door slightly ajar. With his mother not home, this was not normal.

But Martin had not noticed. He had been too intent on getting something to eat; besides the front door had been on his right, the passage opening towards the kitchen area on his left.

There had been no reason to notice anything wrong.

Once inside the cold room, he shivered slightly at the sudden drop in temperature. He found himself a little more alert and present.

At the other end there was a dish of assorted cold meats, and some of his mother's famous coleslaw and pecan-nut salad – another one of his favourites. He could smell it.

He lent forward, placing just enough pressure on the stainless steel wheels of his chair in order to make it to the food on the shelf across the small room itself.

He found it strangely difficult, though. Was something stopping him? Was there an obstacle in front of the wheels? He looked down but could see nothing.

No, it was something else; perhaps not even physical. It was as though there was some force holding him back, trying to prevent him from crossing the room. It was strange, he thought. And he put it down to the turmoil in Tantalis and his hasty return home the night before. He had done this a hundred times; crossed the cold room to fetch some food. How could it suddenly be a problem?

Behind him something quite large moved. It was careful not to reveal itself entirely, and was acutely aware that its smell could easily give it away. It nervously looked down at the floor behind it, then across the kitchen itself and directly at the entrance to the kitchen from the house. Then, turning its head suddenly, it looked at the kitchen door that led to the quart yard. What was it looking for? Someone; something? A quiver, ever so slight, but nevertheless plainly evident (had anyone been looking) rippled up its back and down the side of its ugly face. Its hand curled around the doorway, and for a second it seemed to wince – the cold of the bare steel almost painful to touch. It was facing the back of Martin's wheel-chair, with his head in plain view.

It had a plan.

Martin lent forward and pushed downwards so that the wheels turned once again and allowed his chair to glide gently across the room. His head and shoulders now leant back in order to ensure the right degree of balance. He was determined to get to the cold meat and salads on the far side. The smell of the raw carrot and cabbage, with freshly squeezed lemon juice running through it and over the pecan nuts, permeated the chilly room – he caught it now and it made his mouth water. Was there enough mayonnaise, would he be able to find a bottle of pepper sauce? he wondered.

But he didn't make it.

Two small hands right behind him had already closed tightly over the handle of a large stainless steel pan that had been placed carefully on a shelf high above Martin. The hands had raised the pan as high as they could over the creature's head and they now brought it down with significant force and speed. There was hardly any sound; just a swift and sudden movement as the pan came rushing down, albeit in a very restricted area.

The blow was sudden; the pain, briefly, very briefly, excruciating. Then Martin slumped forward, with a soft whimper. Some long, agonising seconds later he felt the light slip away, his head limp as his body cried out, quite desperately, for air.

Had Martin been conscious he might have heard Magnus announcing his return in the courtyard outside the kitchen door. Had he been conscious, he might have regretted his overdue return. He might have been irritated that he had not been present when he woke up that morning; and he might even have felt somewhat abandoned.

But he was not conscious. Martin slumped forward at such an acute angle that he was in danger of falling out of his chair entirely. His arms slid; the left down the side of his chair; his right forward, down the front of his leg and almost onto the floor in front of him. There was no sign of his large, enticing and friendly brown eyes now. There was no sign of life itself, it seemed.

With the sound of Magnus the creature clearly panicked.

It raised the pan again, not entirely such what to do with it. Perhaps preparing it as a weapon should Magnus come bolting through the flap in the door.

The creature was easily equal in strength to a large human male and perhaps another blow was all that was needed to finish Martin off, it thought. It had a mission, a stated task, and it was not going to return until this was accomplished. The pan was poised, although Martin's head was now no longer clearly in view or an easy target. It raised the pan just a few centimetres above its head in anticipation of the one, final fatal blow.

But then something happened.

Any resolve and courage it might have had when it entered the cold room seemed now to depart, and the muscles on its neck began to quiver quite violently with fear. Its tongue began to flick wildly also.

There were only two things this creature feared the most in the land of humans – dogs and water. Right now, it realised it was in the presence of both. Panicking and with just a split second of doubt about what it should do, it dropped the pan onto the floor and retreated swiftly out of the cold room, closing the door tightly shut behind it.

Within seconds it was gone, leaving behind it just the faint unpleasant smell of its lingering presence.

When Magnus entered the kitchen through his hatch, he was immediately arrested by the foreign smell. Although he had almost certainly never seen the creature before, he was aware that something very unfamiliar to his home had been right there in the kitchen. There was more: it was not only unfamiliar to his home, there was something about it that made Magnus stop and reflect. It was clearly a smell from some far away place, a place of distant memories; another world.

He followed its scent to the door of the cold room; but there was no way inside now. The door was firmly closed. Sadly it would be another twenty minutes of lonely vigil before he could peer inside and see his master and friend.

And what he would see would make him bark with feral anger and hysterical desperation.

He lay down, whining softly, as though in anticipation of the gruesome discovery he would make, knowing that this was where he was meant to be right now.

And Magnus being simply a faithful and loving dog could have no idea that the creature whose smell – this foreign yet strangely familiar scent he could still make out – had been the one responsible for the fourth and final mistake.

After lying beside the closed door for some time, Magnus suddenly remembered where he had detected that smell before.

It had not been anywhere inside their house, but instead outside, and at the bottom of the garden. He began to bark frantically as he hastened towards the open front door.

But the creature had disappeared.

And wherever it had disappeared to, and whatever it was now doing, the creature itself was entirely unaware that this fourth and final mistake would probably cost it its life.

::: fourteen :::

The Gathering of Storm Clouds

in limine
at the threshold

Morduainé knew that Diablo would seek glory out in the open.

There would be no scurrying around in the Dark Woods, or stealthy ambushes from behind trees. He would march his troops of Inkwas and the smattering of bad trolls onto the Soft Plains and there to make a stand for all to see.

Morduainé feared for his elves. Even though he knew the collective energies of the Universe were behind them, they were not physically as strong as the average Inkwa. Their main forte in combat, something they had not entered into for aeons, was the bow and arrow. And then short armed combat with swords lovingly made by the trolls – these were short, stabbing weapons that could bring anything down at close range.

The Inkwas, on the other hand had long spears and were able to launch them, albeit with their short arms, with tremendous force, and throw them over long distances. Would this overwhelm the elves? Would a quick, early attack unnerve the allies of Tantalis? How much death would there be? Morduainé shivered – the thought of it made him lose his resolve for a fleeting second.

In one sense, though, Diablo was playing into his hands by marching onto the Soft Plains. It could only be his arrogance forcing him to do this – combat under a forest canopy would have been far more tricky for the allies of Tantalis and her queen, and definitely in Diablo's favour.

But then again on the plains – this meant that dragones could marshal an attack from the air, dropping their 'blood' directly onto them, and also sweeping down in order to fire-ball them (although a particularly dangerous manoeuvre for the dragones themselves). Then there was the secret weapon of the faeries, also not easily executed or delivered inside a forest, and far more suited to an open expanse. No, things had definitely played into their hands.

It was this that boosted Morduainé's confidence.

"Do you think you will be ready?" asked Queen Fara. She was clearly troubled and moved the fingers of her left hand round and round inside that of her right, something Morduainé had not seen her do before. He nodded.

"It is going to be something of a shock for both sides, I think," he said. "Even though the art remains embedded within us, and we often play games and watch previous battles through the Console, being there and engaging in real combat is going to be something relatively new for many.

I've no doubt we will muster the courage and abilities needed – Dragone's Essence and our rehabilitation to Atlantis is not just a possibility, it is a certainty," he concluded.

"I know," said Queen Fara, "this I am convinced of. But I am used to facing almost any other obstacle apart from that of open combat and war. It has been such a long time." Her thoughts trailed off, and Morduainé waited patiently for his queen to gather them again. "Even the banishment and chaos of humans leaving, their anger, their vengeful slaying of dragones so long ago; it's somewhat real, yet so far away in time. I don't often think about it anymore. I was very young."

"I remember it also, Fara," said Morduainé touching her hand gently. "But we have had the bad trolls to contend with, and there have been many skirmishes with the Inkwish over the centuries. I do not think we will have forgotten entirely how to fight. In fact I am quite confident we shall prevail." Morduainé realised his words were clearly a comfort to himself also.

"Do you think the bad trolls will play a decisive role?" asked Queen Fara.

"No," said Morduainé confidently. "Remember, there are only a few of them left, and their role is traditionally one of support rather than engagement. I foresee open combat only with

Inkwas. It is clear that Diablo is no longer playing the role of troublemaker; he has managed to evoke a particularly cruel and vengeful force this time. He is no longer taunting us. This time he means to destroy."

Queen Fara listened carefully to Morduainé and then made her own observations: "I am informed by Elfin Watchers and also by a number of faeries who have returned from the human world that there is particular danger between some nations at the moment. There are powerful individuals who seek the destruction of the Circle, of innocent life and property. It seems to have gone far beyond political wrangling and power-play; there are leaders who speak openly of world war once again."

She shook her head from side to side, thinking deeply, and then continued:

"I think that you are right, Morduainé. Diablo has managed to elicit a particular strain of evil from somewhere, as you clearly point out. What is strange to me is that he seems no longer content to unleash it upon humankind, but has brought it into *our* midst."

"You are forgetting one thing, Fara ..." She looked at him, trying hard to focus. Morduainé continued: "It is, in fact, we who have brought the focus and attention into our midst in the form of Martin. The real battle is now here, and things have been re-

190

versed.

Whereas before Inkwas used humans and their problems to reflect and bare the brunt of their own evil intent, it is now our turn. It seems we here in Tantalis will this time carry the burden of war and malevolence that rises from humans themselves. The battle for the rehabilitation of humankind has now begun, and the first decisive moves for its success will be made tomorrow on the Soft Plains."

"I shall enter the Great Hall with sadness this evening, Morduainé," said Queen Fara. Morduainé simply nodded, understanding the heaviness she felt. It was not unusual for an elfin queen to carry with her the burden of her people, and even that of the entire Tantalis. At times even hearing their cries, listening to their secret fears and the collective pain, borne over aeons since the separation from the human world, deep within herself.

Edytya and Kyla came to her side, each one taking her hand and they led her to her private courtyard. She had not asked them to do so, but she walked with them now, her eyes closed, content to be led, to be cared for while she tried to focus away from the hurtful past, and the anxiety of what might go wrong the next day. Instead she tried to focus on the Now and its power she was so easily able to rely on under normal circumstances.

They undressed her, and after running their hands down her body in an attitude of removing the dark thoughts and influences from her head, through her thighs, and out at her feet, they guided her into the large pool, thick and almost boiling with herbs and fragrant leaves.

Fara immediately felt better and she let her head fall backwards. Kyla took hold of it, brushing her long hair to one side and resting it in her own lap as she sat down; she began to sing Fara's favourite song – that of Atlantis rising again and the groaning of the Earth coming to an end. She could detect the soft gentle hum of accompaniment by Fara herself.

Edytya worked at Fara's feet, washing and massaging them dexterously; her long, thin fingers working nimbly between each toe, using just enough pressure to release the tension deep within her queen's body. She too sang softly, looking up now and then at Fara, looking for any sign of disturbance or displeasure.

Kyla closed her eyes and took a long, deep breath; she then raised both her hands and, turning them so that her thumbs faced downwards, she wiped both her eyes from the inside outwards, curling her two thumbs upwards so as to catch the liquid her eyes exuded; with this she rubbed Fara's forehead gently. Special Attending Elfins had the ability to secrete an essence that acted like a balm: it was creamy and rich once it came into contact with elfin skin, and Kyla worked it in slowly, her fingers circling in opposite directions. This was a special gift young Attending Elfin girls were able to offer, especially to women they loved; yet a gift that diminished over time, as they got older.

Fara sighed deeply, loving every minute of the attention she was receiving; she found herself drifting off to sleep, but somewhere between the structure of organised thought and the dreaminess of letting go, she suddenly sensed something quite powerful; she sat up, her face showing clearly that she was disturbed. Kyla nodded to Edytya, who got up and summoned a faery from the adjoining room immediately. When she entered, Queen Fara spoke:

"There is something wrong with Martin. Please arrange for a Watcher to return now; tell Jezze-B to access the Console in case there is someone already nearby. They should remain with him."

The faery nodded and then flew quickly between the tall granite columns in the room, out through the door and into the courtyard.

Queen Fara relaxed once again, looking up at Kyla and indicating that she should continue. The time she spent with them was her own personal privilege; no one entered her room without consulting the faery guard first and she was always confident of being able to escape in her private quarters. And something told her that she would need all the attention right now; her alignment would have to be strong and balanced. Without any doubt she knew that the days ahead would test and try all of them to their individual and collective limits.

She looked up into Kyla's eyes, and wondered what she herself was going through. She raised her hand and stroked Kyla's hair, and then watched as she closed her eyes in response to her gentle touch.

Only Phantoam landed in the Great Hall later that evening.

The other dragones, fearful of more attacks and in order to be ready in position, had flown to their maximum height and now hovered there, some even sleeping to preserve as much energy as possible. They would probably remain there all night.

The Console indicated that Diablo would assemble early the next morning, which meant the dragones were right. Morduainé addressed the assembly, few members of which had anything to say – there was no disagreement, no contention of overriding anxiety; only a strong sense of collective ability, purpose and of the Now. And that Now was the absolute repelling of Diablo and his beasts, and the return of Martin so they could march to Dragone's Lair behind the waterfall.

Morduainé reiterated this again, allowing the Console to

conjure up the image and project it around the Great Hall. The sound of rushing water and the thunderous waterfall itself filled the room, so that some of the trolls even held up their hands in anticipation of getting wet.

In their gentle manner, it was always necessary to laugh at something, and this they now did although the laughter itself was not of the usual kind, and it subsided quickly.

It was clear; it was simple: one task completed, a new one would begin. The final goal: the Lair and the opening of the Box. They could no longer prolong this event. Everything that was happening made this apparent, and Morduainé found it quite unnecessary to verbalise this essential goal. He merely looked around the room, feeling, seeing, sensing the agreement and purpose projected towards him from each person present. Phantoam was the only one who said anything: "We know what is to be done, Morduainé."

Around the Hall a great hum of unison hung in the air, like the prolonged harmony of a chorus. And then it was time.

The night was long, thick with anticipation and pride; a little uncertainty. The sounds of birds were everywhere, and then suddenly none, as though they too were taking time off to prepare for the dreadful event. Elves and trolls sat next to one another, or lay down in groups. And all the night Queen Fara moved around, Kyla and Edytya beside her, Fara holding their hands.

She stopped to soothe the troubled spirit of a troll who was crying, and then there were more who needed her special presence. She knew it would be a long night.

Trollip said nothing when she walked past, but looking into her eyes he knew that something was amiss with Martin; he sensed death and wondered whether this meant his own, or that of his friend.

Fara stooped to touch him on the shoulder, and as his head fell to the side, as though in anticipation of his cheek brushing against his queen's hand, she unfurled her long fingers across his face and placed him into a deep sleep.

On and on she walked. How many there were, from all corners of the palace and the settlements beyond? Young, old, some well over five hundred years in age. Trolls unsightly, trolls quaint – she discovered one as young as twenty and sent him home immediately. By the early morning she must have ministered to more than five thousand of all types needing her, and then she fell to the ground, under a tree and slept, with Kyla and Edytya at her side.

It was a sleep that would last a long time, away from the danger, the agony and the terror of combat itself although she would later experience her own frustration in having to stay in her palace while her subjects fought for all that she and Tantalis held true.

In fact so deep was her sleep that she missed, the following morning, the sound of soft trumpets, the flutter-drone of some five hundred faeries hovering just off the ground; the spongy butter-light of the early morning that filtered through her windows and danced on the floor of her chamber. She missed, also, the somewhat sharper than usual rays of the sun striking the buildings and rocks around them outside. And the rousing of thousands; the gentle clatter of their weapons and the constant munching of olives by at least two thousand trolls.

She would miss, in fact, the general flutter, the obsessive fiddling with buttons, belts, weapons and even with one another, as the throng of Tantalians prepared, nervously, to go to war, knowing instinctively that their destiny awaited them across the kingdom, right in the middle of the Soft Plains itself.

::: fifteen :::
Diablo

ohe! jam satis …
Oh! That is enough …

The Inkwa returned.

Diablo was at first pleased to see him and greeted him with relish, full of the plans for battle, red tongued and red faced and with the full flush of excitement at impending victory.

But it was short-lived.

When the Inkwa, Daelops, told him of his ordeal, Diablo went quite berserk.

He swore violently, shaking Daelops with both hands until the Inkwa quivered in abject fear, against the side of the cave.

"You idiot! You fool! You were told to bring him back here. Fasthikut! Fasthikut! I will kill you myself. I had prepared for him a special treat – do you see this hole? Do you see it? Did I not show it to you? Are you blind as well as stupid?"

Daelops began to quiver; he could clearly see the look in Diablo's eyes. He had thought he might convince him of another plan. Perhaps he could return, perhaps Martin had not been so important after all. After all he *had* killed him – surely that was all that was important? He was incredulous when he looked,

198

again, into Diablo's eyes. He knew instinctively that he was also doomed.

Diablo could not contain himself any longer and leant backwards onto his hindquarters, into a traditional Inkwa stance of attack, his tail erect and ready.

And then he spiralled forward, turning his body sideways at the last second, the attack itself blindingly fast.

Daelops could only cringe in anticipation of the blow that came like a knife through butter: the sharp, razor-edge of Diablo's carefully groomed diamond shaped tail-end sliced into his face, and tore his cheek wide open. The green blood splayed against the rock-face of the cave, and Daelops cried out in desperate pain. Yet even from the depths of fear he was able to summon a plea:

"I did what you told me – to deal with him; I could not bring him back – there was a dog; a human dog! Please understand, Oursth. Pleeeasth, forgive me." He held his tiny hands up against the side of his face, the blood gushing outwards, through his fingers, and down his face.

"You did what I told you? You fasthikut whimpering peasant! I told you to capture him – what good is he to me dead!?"

Daelops tried one more time, little knowing that each word, each syllable was simply a step towards the inevitable. "He is no longer a threat now – this is what you wanted, surely, Oursth?"

"A threat? A threat?" Diablo moved so that his forced breath made the green oozing blood move to one side. "Of course he is a threat; but I wanted him *here* to bargain with. You fool!"

And then it didn't seem to matter any more and he backed off, taking a long hard looked at Daelops. At first Daelops thought that this was it; perhaps Diablo had reconciled the inevitable, had forgiven him, perhaps he had changed his mind. He even started to smile.

But then Diablo shifted his thick tail once again. And with one swift movement he knocked the whimpering Inkwa into the hole.

Daelops immediately scrambled around, digging up fresh earth to plaster his face, knowing that it would heal the gaping wound – a power the Inkwish inherited from their previous elfin state.

But it was all to be in vain.

Diablo sat down, now seemingly calm, next to the hole his workers had dug so feverishly, and breathed deeply. When he let the air out his lungs, he relaxed completely; his heartbeat having dropped dramatically so that it was no more than twenty beats a minute.

But Daelops, having now given up all hope, knew what was to come and cried out in utter desperation, trying to shield himself and yet trying, also, not to make his attempt to escape too obvious. He knew the final punishment would only be worse if he hid himself, or refused in some way to take his master's vitriol.

The glands deep in Diablo's throat throbbed and thumped against his large windpipe, swelling so that his whole face looked distorted and outrageously grotesque.

Still his heart hardly beat at all and his breathing was precise and even.

And then with deadly accuracy Diablo spat the two fluids outwards into the air and down at his victim.

His aim was perfect, and the fluids landed at the same time and on the same square inch of skin on Daelops' head, cheeks, arms and hindquarters. Each time, Diablo made a sighing sound as he gathered the energy and strength to shoot the deadly chemicals so that they would mix at landing, precisely, and eat right through Daelops' thick scaly skin.

All through the night the wail of Daelops' torment made the four thousand Inkwas assembled outside shake with fear.

Some of the younger ones embarrassed themselves by

urinating uncontrollably; unable to contain their terror.

Their only respite was that Diablo was venting his wrath on only one of them, and they could only hope that tomorrow he would turn his vengeance more directly toward their enemy.

But still, every now and then a young Inkwa would begin to wail, and Armai or Geaddon would have to find some way of consoling them.

::: sixteen :::
The Sky Is Dark

ora pro nobis
pray for us

Morning has broken. The queen is awake. The soft light is now gone: no dancing or swirling of buttery light on her chamber floor: all beauty, all energy seems to have been summoned to another place. Few, if any are present to comfort her. Later she will venture into the Great Hall to witness her victory through the Console.

But there is no joy in the palace now.

The Great Hall stands empty, forlorn, silent; the waters of the courtyards stop. Birds abate.

Queen Fara retreats with Kyla to her resting-room, to prepare herself for victory. It is not the thought of defeat that saddens her and abruptly halts the flow of abundant life here. It is the presence of imminent danger – the flow, itself, of death; of blood, pain. Ever increasing pain, so long forgotten.

It is the thought of a real, present and evil enemy Fara had long since buried deep within her spirit. Is this the price? she thinks as she walks; can humankind not move one inch towards their common goal of restoration and rehabilitation by themselves? Why is it that, always, another must pay their price?

Far from the palace there is the drone of thousands marching.

The buzz-hum singing of the fearies led by Jezze-B, eager, agile and full of the flush of anticipation, fills the air.

They are more confident now and in just a few hours they will be there.

The majestic hills are brushed with verdant green and punctuated by rocky faces. The marchers are kept busy recognising familiar figures. When they look up they recognise Phantoam, his huge body beautifully carved in the rock-face itself: he smiles at them. Queen Fara appears, subdued, but also smiling, with Kyla at her side. Some of the faeries fly up towards the cliffs without realising how large the images are, and that getting there might take a long time. Jezze-b irritatingly calls them back. Trol-lip laughs at a throng of trolls appearing through a thicket in what can only be a representation of the Dark Woods. He recognises himself and sticks his chest out proudly, making sure those around him have seen the image too.

The army sings songs: the elves in perfect harmony; the songs of the trolls are slightly more suited to the human world, perhaps; that sung in a pub or a sporting stadium. The faeries sing in forgotten languages, with musical timing they invent as they go along so that, to humans, the music would sound alternative. Many of the trolls are irritated by this, and sing their own songs even louder.

Morduainé rides with two aides, making sure they do not push the majestic and eager tricorns too hard, or themselves too far. There is no eagerness to die, no eagerness to entice anyone into anger, and ever mindful of the balance of energy, they make sure they are strong, and focussed with the power of the Now filtering through them from their surroundings.

As the hills come to an end, and the waterfalls begin to subside, Morduainé orders them to stop, drink, rest and prepare for their entrance through a narrow valley, and onto the plains. Scouts return on tricornback to say the plain is empty. The Inkwas have gathered on the other side, out of range and sight, amongst the scrub and trees and across the wide plain itself.

It is another hour before they are assembled. The trolls are in front, and in a flanking position also. The bulk of the elves are behind them in rows of about three hundred each – they are taller and there find themselves free to launch their arrows. It is also a tactical consideration in that should the trolls lose their swords, elves can replenish them with theirs.

The faeries keep to the ground behind the elves; theirs is the first surprise attack, and will soon prove to be one of the most troublesome and damaging to the Inkwish. They carry with them a secret weapon, and carefully tend it at their feet, stroking it, talking to it, enticing their charge to produce its secret fluid, as would the moth that feeds off it. The flower itself perhaps detecting the difference between the touch of a faery and that of a moth, is at first reluctant.

Finally they are ready.

Over the gentle hill, some distance away on the other side the Inkwish arrive. There is no parley, no hesitation or doubt; they all seem to understand what must be done, and in all respects this is traditional war, fought for centuries in the human world, with the one side facing the other. It was what came naturally to them, although they had lived without it for centuries. It was a simple war without the electronic technology harnessed by humans so that they may be far away and still kill at a whim.

There are to be some surprises, though.

Inkwas form battle groups in the centre, with others that flank the main group on either side, and then there is large support from far behind. Who knows what is over the hill. The elves cannot see. Yet many have forgotten the obvious and just how many Inkwas there are, but soon everyone will know the full extent of the Inkwa force – their numbers and position.

This will be even clearer when the dragones arrive.

There is almost a calm; not one Inkwa moves; settled in tight formations or companies of around one hundred, they squat on their tails, sometimes allowing the tips to curl around them so they can fondle or stroke them gently.

Morduainé is on his tricorn in front; behind him the trusted trolls, low on the ground, ready to rise only when the enemy is close enough. They carry no shields like the elves, but for all their loping gate and cumbersome ways, they too hold a secret weapon.

A gentle breeze blows, first Morduainé's hair, so that its tips brush his cheeks and then, as if the air itself has a mission, it meanders over the heads of the elves, cooling them from the heat of the sun.

Two central divisions part slightly, thereby moving closer to those that are flanking them. At first it is not clear why they have moved left and right; something is happening. The elves shift slightly from side to side, tension within them mounting. The trolls, low down, groan and quiver with expectation, uncertainty.

Someone is walking between the two divisions. When he clears their ranks and finally comes out into the open and slightly down the slope, it is easy to see who it is.

It is Diablo.

All is quiet; hushed.

He is taller than anyone else behind him. He holds his spear in his right hand. His small shield is held in his left – it is as strong as three inches of steel, light as aluminium, and glistens in the mid-morning sun. He holds it, trying to reflect the sun towards the enemy across the plain but the light is not strong enough and the shield not reflective enough, and it does not work.

As he breathes in and out, his throat makes a rough grunting sound, first arbitrarily, then rhythmically, so that it sounds like a drum beat. It gets louder and louder. The elves can almost hear it. The Inkwas behind him certainly can and the sound excites them so that they shift from one foot to another in anticipation.

Diablo stands up fully erect, his shield raised in front of his body on the one side, his spear on the other. The company behind him rises too, instantly – an ancient calling, an instinctive reaction.

Diablo opens his mouth.

This time the elves can hear him clearly.

And it is a sound and a cry they have not heard before:

"KGAAAAA! **Boem**-a-Sukka!"

Silence settles like a thick blanket, for a second time.

There is a long pause, and then again:

"KGAAAAAAAAAAAAAA! **Boem**-a-Sukka!"

As the word *boem* is shouted, they bang their spears against their shields so as to heighten the effect of the thunderously sounding word itself. It is so effective, the faeries uncharacteristically fall back behind the elves.

There is a pause and the company behind Diablo in the centre bang their spears together against their shields. They do this exactly like a Zulu Impie battalion would do in order to instil fear in their opponent. They rattle them against the secret metal in their shields they stole from the elves; it has a special tonic resonance to it that is quite beautiful, and as it resonates louder, quite eerily and intimidatingly it makes a kind of Rrrrrrrmmmpp-PHHA! that sounds like a cymbal right at the end.

The faeries quiver.

Jezze-B let's out a hiss, half admonishing, half calming her company, some of which have fallen too far back behind their front line.

But it is just the beginning and Diablo starts again. This time the rhythm begins, and his war-cry takes some structured form, with the cymbal-like sound of the spears against the shields coming immediately thereafter.

"KGAAAAAAAAAAAAAAAA !

Zoem-a-Sukka, **Zoem**-a-Sukka

KWA-KWA-KWA !

Zoem-a-Sukka, **Zoem**-a-Sukka

CHA-CHA-CHA !

Zoem-a-Sukka, **Zoem**-a-Sukka !

Kwa-Kwa-Kwa !

You **are**; We **are**

the **IN-IN-**KWAAA !"

And then the sound of their spears against their shields:
Rrrrrrmmmpp-PHHA!

Diablo repeats this three times, louder each time; then
with one small movement of his hand, the battalion behind him
squats down again, and the two flanking battalions rise. It is like
a well choreographed ballet.

On the left they, too, raise their spears and shields, but the
sound they make is quite different, and the rhythm is also new,
obscure, and rousing in a frightening way. On the left the deep
thudding sound of the spears against the shields, now very different to the cymbal-like sound before, and which sounds something like this:

DU-DU. Du-du-du !

And then the far-right battalion replies:

Du-du, du-du. Du-Du !

This they do from left to right another three times, and then there is silence once again. Then the first, central battalion rises once more and repeats the first opening beat:

DU-DU, du-du-du!

Without rising, the entire army of Inkwas reply with the matching rhythm, becoming familiar to everyone, and as rousing as any war-cry there could be: Du-du, du-du. DU-DU!

The sounds fill the entire plain, and echo off the rock face in the valleys beyond. Only Morduainé does not move a muscle, but stares straight at Diablo, some distance away.

Diablo leans forward and, in an obscene gesture, spits his poison at Morduainé, knowing full well it will not come even close to him.

And then, without warning, the first battalion of Inkwas, as swiftly as a Phisteriss rushing through the scrub, rises, leans backwards and hurls their spears high, straight and with deadly accuracy.

The long spears come like an angry torrent. Up, and then down, down. But the Inkwas have made an error by throwing at the frontline where the trolls alone are crouching. The trolls awaken from the mesmerising effect of the rhythmical beat only just in time, and they scurry into position so as to be able to judge the path of the spears' descent.

Their secret weapon is one of pure defence.

For all their awkward, loping gait and ungainly appearance, they posses the keenest, most agile skills. Their eyes so sharp, their balance so finely tuned, their accurate perception and judgement so far advanced, that it is unlikely that any spear will find its way to them. Their vision locks onto its target and at the last second they are able to jump out of the way. It is one of the reasons they carry no shields; only their trusted swords.

The spears fall mostly on dead ground as the trolls scurry this way and that. Three spears, only, fall further than the rest and catch two elves, one on the leg, the other directly in the chest. The wounds open like burst seed pods, and the elves fall amongst their companions who rush to their aid.

The trolls are unable to throw the spears back at this range, but gather them quickly and hand them to the elves immediately behind them. There is silence again.

Morduainé raises one arm. His tricorn stamps, its head held high, with nostrils pumping like a blacksmith's bellows. Down comes his arm and those behind him spring into action.

The second line of elves draws its arrows from the slings of the first, and directly in front of it. Their movement is extremely swiftly and in one blurred but efficient movement they launch the arrows. And the sound is a clear **Sssshhoeffffffff**!

The tiny missiles rocket through the air but unlike normal arrows that follow an upward trajectory and then come raining down, the elves have some way of making sure each arrow follows a very straight path across the plain towards the front line. But the arrows will not find their mark, for the Inkwish have their shields and know how to use them, holding them in a tortoise-like formation in front of them so as to make the outer skin of their company almost impenetrable.

The arrows serve only as a diversion, offering the Inkwish false security. The elves know this and do not waste energy feeling in any way inferior in that their efforts fall literally on bare ground.

They wait patiently and without turning to see, they know that right behind them more than three hundred faeries rise over the heads of their fellow elves and trolls and fly towards the enemy; themselves as straight as arrows. When they reach the Inkwish they hover just out of reach. The Inkwas have no arrows, but only their swords and spears and they desperately jab at the air, trying to reach the irritating creatures above them. Of course their shields are still in front of them, now many on the ground; the Inkwas do not know what is to come, or have simply forgotten, and do not raise their valuable and necessary shields as protection.

Jezze-B and her companions taunt them mercilessly, and Diablo himself tries to climb on the shoulders of another Inkwa in an attempt to reach her. He hurls his spear upwards, but it simply falls to the ground right next to him. The faeries' presence is somewhat unsettling to the Inkwas who sense that something is about to happen.

It is indeed time for the faeries; and their secret weapon is revealed.

Just when they have drawn the attention of the Inkwas below them, they hold the Weeping Moth Flower, downwards, tickling its base. Within seconds the flower ejaculates its precious seed – the most nutritious substance in Tantalis (to the Weeping Moth), but nothing less than deadly on skin of any kind. The strong ejaculatory projection, coupled with the force of gravity means that the liquid reaches the Inkwas' faces and eyes almost instantly.

The entire battalion falls to the ground, moaning; their eyes blind, their skin on fire. It is almost as putrid as the poison from another Inkwa. They scream with pain, patting and beating themselves and one another – their efforts, of course, only making the pain worse as they rub the fiery liquid deeper into their skin.

The faeries retreat, not one of them harmed. And it is at

this point that the elves launch another salvo of arrows. But not following a straight path; instead they shoot them upwards and allow them to follow a traditional trajectory so that they will land from above.

They find their mark this time. There are no shields, only arms and legs flailing frantically in a pathetic attempt to alleviate the fire of the Weeping Moth Flower's seed. More than half the battalion falls to the ground, some wounded, many dead, the arrow-heads themselves having been carefully soaked in the deadly poison.

Diablo cries out in pain himself, but more in frustration. His anger gets the better of him and he runs forward, his sword drawn, calling two flanking battalions, one led by Armai and another by Geaddon to follow – about two hundred and fifty Inkwas. He is some distance away, but the thunderous thump of their large hind legs is daunting.

The Inkwas run sideways, as though descending a steep slope and, when at full gallop, they lean back onto their tails that give them added balance and a spring action, propelling them further forward. This awkward looking gait means that unless they stop dead, their bellies are almost fully exposed.

The trolls creep forward now, almost flat between the long grass, undetected, scurrying quickly to get into position some distance away from their front-line.

Diablo comes nearer and nearer, the two flanking battalions converging right behind him. At the last minute the trolls, risking their lives with the full force of the Inkwas almost on top of them, rise and aim for their unprotected bellies, just beneath their shields.

It is as if the Inkwas have run straight into a barbed wire fence. The trolls' swords pierce them in their underside, in their thighs; some trolls, who bravely manage to stand fully erect plunge their weapons deep into their attackers' hearts, beneath their armpits and to the one side of their protective shields.

It is unprecedented slaughter.

The trolls cough and splutter from the thick mush of Inkwa blood running down their cheeks and into their mouths. Some of the wounded and dead Inkwas fall onto the trolls who struggle to release themselves under their superior weight.

Diablo takes a hit. Trollip himself waits for him, eyeing each movement he makes carefully, hoping to find the precise moment for attack, but at the last minute another Inkwa brushes past and knocks Trollip down, allowing him to land only a perfunctory blow to Diablo's leg.

Those Inkwas not wounded make a hasty retreat, and it leaves them breathless as they have to retreat up an incline.

It is left to the remaining trolls in the second line to come forward and without hesitation to make sure every Inkwa on the ground is killed. This they do with unexpressed delight, but it is a relish they will later regret as the whole of Tantalis will suffer the burden in some way or another.

In the palace, far away, Queen Fara shudders as a bitter cold sense of death permeates her like an icy wind through a thin and bare forest.

Diablo retreats.

Eventually all is quiet. Having backed off, he is some distance away, talking to his troops. Soon they retreat even further, almost as far as the hilltop on the other side.

For a while there is some relative silence again – the faeries, trolls and elves regroup, reposition, placate one another; and whisper orders, encouragement and hope within their circle.

And it is at this moment that Phantoam appears high up with a horde of dragones. Some elves shiver in anticipation, knowing what is to come. A few younger trolls have never seen so many dragones before, least of all in the air and tremble, a little, at the very sight.

The sky is thick with their coming; the sky is dark.

Yet it is not the arrival of Phantoam and his troop that amazes those on the plains, or even catches their attention.

It is the arrival of someone quite unexpected that will shake Tantalis and redirect its path forever.

::: seventeen :::
Escape

dies faustus
a lucky day

Mrs Fields did not return in time.

It was Dominika who found the front door open and Magnus frantically barking at the door of the cold room.

She walked through the house, knowing that something was wrong; sensing it, feeling it, yet missing the drama itself.

"What is it Magnus?" she asked over and over. He barked and barked and barked. Each time he returned to the kitchen and the door of the cold room, but Dominika simply looked at him and shook her head. Why on earth would he be barking at the cold room? she asked herself.

And then it dawned on her. "Are you hungry? What do you want inside the cold room? Come on Magnus, where's everybody?"

She walked to the door and opened it.

There was Martin, slumped forward, as cold as ice, as blue as an iceberg floating in the sea. At first she recoiled, fighting her own panic. Magnus did not stop his barking and jumped up against Martin's wheelchair again and again, trying to rouse his

219

master.

"Oh, my God! Oh my God! What-the .... Martin! Martin, what happened!" She reached out and felt his head; it was cold. She tried to negotiate his chair back through the door, and banged her fingers and hands against the door frame, again and again. Eventually she managed to get the chair free and into the passage, and then into the main body of the kitchen itself.

She tugged at him, until he fell to the floor. By this time she was crying, frantic, desperately trying to remember what she would have to do to revive him. Was he dead, was he just unconscious, how long had he been there?

He lay on his side, stiff, on the bare floor of the kitchen.

Dominika pulled him over onto his back. And then suddenly all her first-aid training came to her, and she tried as hard as she could to calm herself. She placed her hand under his neck, raising his face towards her and upwards, opening his windpipe. And then she opened his mouth. Only for a split second did she hesitate; then lowered her own mouth over his and blew gently. Nothing happened.

She blew again. Nothing happened. And then she blew harder and harder, until she could feel a very slight, gentle movement of his chest against her flat hand.

Was he breathing?

"Come on Martin, come on! Damn you. I'm sorry! I'm sorry ..." She began to cry, her tears falling onto his face and down his cheeks through her open fingers that held his head.

Nothing.

She blew and blew and blew. Eventually her own breath, through his mouth, began to warm him and make his chest move up and down. She did not stop, remembering her training: *continue until a doctor arrives.*

Oh, my God, a doctor! she thought to herself. She got up off the floor and grabbed the telephone, dialling the emergency number. And then back. Blow; count; blow; count. Her hands on his chest desperate for any sign of movement from his lungs. Blow; count: was there something? Did his chest move by itself, or was it just her imagination?

Some minutes later an ambulance arrived, but not before she could hear the sound of a Renault's engine in the driveway also.

She was still blowing, and Martin's chest was now starting to move rhythmically. Up and down, up and down; but Dominika had no way of knowing whether it was her own or Martin's breath that was making his chest rise and fall.

And just before anyone could enter the house, he coughed. The colour suddenly returned to his face and he coughed again, spluttering and heaving. He tried to sit up, but was unable to do so by himself.

Mrs Fields came bursting in through the door.

By this time Martin was sitting up with Dominika's help; his eyes only just partially open.

"Oohh … oh!" he groaned, turning sideways, and then lifting his hand towards his head.

"What's going on?!" shouted Mrs Fields.

"I don't know," said Dominika, "I arrived and found him in the cold room."

"In the cold room? Why's he on the floor? Martin, Martin!" She knelt down and held his head in her arms. "What happened, what happened? Are you alright?"

"Yes, mother," he said, "it's my head … so sore …"

"Get him to his bed," she said to Dominika. "No, back into his chair. We won't be able to carry him."

Just then the paramedics came through the kitchen door. They were in time to help Martin into his chair and wheel him into his room, laying him on his bed. They examined him extensively, with both Mrs Fields and Dominika looking on, wondering what could have happened.

"I think he's going to be okay, but we've called a doctor just in case."

"He's obviously had a bad knock on the head, and might suffer from concussion; the doctor will be here shortly. We'll wait with you."

"Concussion – what on earth … ?"

Both Mara and Dominika ran to the cold room; when they got there they found the heavy stainless steel pan on the floor.

Back in the room they sat on the bed with Martin and waited for the doctor.

Another six minutes, perhaps seven, and she arrived.

"Thank you." The doctor turned to the ambulance crew, and then to Mrs Fields, she said: "There is no question about it, he must go to hospital right now for observation."

"No!" said Martin unfalteringly, "I know what happened, I am going to be just fine. I just want to lie here and rest; I'm not going anywhere."

"It'll only be for a day or two, perhaps not even that," said the doctor.

"I understand," he said looking into her eyes, "but I don't want to go. Please don't make me," said Martin groaning a little from the pain of the blood rushing through his hands.

"If he thinks he's okay, you won't have to worry about caring for him," said Mrs Fields. "The two of us won't leave his side – that I promise!"

The doctor shook her head. "You don't understand, it was quite a substantial blow – look here." She parted his hair to reveal the damage. "Only observation and tests will show us what damage there might be."

"I can do the tests tomorrow," said Martin slowly and somewhat groggily. "I'm comfortable here and can take better care of myself. I know what to do; nurses won't. Can you see that I'm a paraplegic?"

The doctor looked down at his legs, suddenly taken aback.

"No, I didn't know." She hesitated, a little embarrassed. She turned to Mara and Dominika. "Will you agree to my coming tomorrow first thing tomorrow to take a look?"

"Yes," said Martin. "I promise I'll be fine." And then he fell back onto his pillow from exhaustion.

The doctor looked at Mara and also at Dominika. "When you say you won't leave his side, do you mean it?"

"Absolutely," they both said.

"Okay, it's very much against my better judgement I must tell you. But if that's what you all want, it might be better for you to take care of him in his own environment. I'll be calling first thing on my way to rounds tomorrow, around seven thirty. Please don't wake him for me, just let him sleep. Will you phone me if *anything* changes?"

"Yes, doctor. Yes, we promise. Thank you," said Mrs Fields.

They walked her down the passage, and through the sitting room to the front door.

"If it is concussion, you should be looking out for headaches that won't go away and especially nausea. Here's my card and number. Only one of you should be here showing me out, anyway," she said pointing a finger. "Now get back to him and keep your promise – someone there the whole night, okay?"

"Yes. Thank you very much."

They closed the door, looked at one another and hurried back to the room. Both the doctor and the ambulance pulled out of the driveway.

They were alone and when they reached Martin he was fast asleep, his breathing regular and deep. He was as peaceful as if nothing had happened.

His colour had returned fully, with only a large blue patch on the side of his head that blended well with the blue patterns on his pillow case.

Dominika began to cry and Mara held her tightly against her chest until her sobs subsided into quiet and gentle breathing also.

Later that evening Martin woke. He could sense someone

was in the room, and turned to see who it was. It was Dominika. They were both suddenly embarrassed at the eye contact.

"Did you find me?" asked Martin, after a long silence. Dominika nodded.

"You saved my life?"

"Probably not," said Dominika sleepily, and quite exhausted herself. "The doctor said you must have been breathing all the time. You must have been in there for a long time, she said."

"About twenty minutes," said Martin after another silence between them. "I didn't fall or anything. It was someone from behind who hit me."

Dominika put her plate down. "What do you mean? Who would want to do that to you!?"

Again Martin was silent for some time and then: "I don't know for sure, but I have a strong feeling it was an Inkwa."

Dominika was incredulous. She held her hands up against her mouth. "You can't tell Mara that; she simply won't understand. And they will *definitely* put you in hospital if you start talking about faeries and Inkwas! Surely you know *that.*"

"Yes, I know; I'm not stupid," said Martin resignedly.

Dominika sighed deeply and shook her head. This had to be the lowest point, she thought to herself. "Are you hungry?"

Martin suddenly realised he had had nothing to eat all day. "Yes," he said.

Dominika returned with a plate, and a smiling Mara at his door. He ate reasonably well, but without finishing everything.

"I'm going to sleep on the floor on a mattress," said Dominika. Martin nodded. They were quiet for a long time and then when his mother was gone, Martin said:

"Are you going to come back?"

Dominika looked up at her friend, a little embarrassed, and then quickly down at her feet. There was silence between them again. Dominika wanted to say so much, to apologize, to explain; she felt lost. Eventually a few tears welled up in her eyes:

"I went wild when I found you in the cold room. I can't tell you how I felt ... I was so sorry about what I did at school, and I said sorry over and over. I really meant it, Martin. I was so afraid of being caught out, and having everyone laugh at me. The only way I could deal with it was to imagine it was all a dream."

"But it wasn't a dream," said Martin, "and I have a mission and I want you ..." Dominika interrupted him:

"It's *your* mission, and you have to continue. I don't really feel I belong there ..."

"I thought we were in this together …" The tone of Martin's voice showed the sadness he felt more than did the look on his face.

Dominika said nothing at first. She didn't want to turn her back on Martin again, but she didn't think she could go back either. Tantalis was just too much. She began to pull the mattress out from under Martin's bed.

"There is no way you can go back; you simply can't, not now; especially not after what you said just now. You must be crazy to even think of going back." What Dominika was saying was as much a practical consideration as it was something she was saying in her own defence.

Martin's mother suddenly appeared at the door. "Go back where?" she asked.

"Oh! … go back? Go back to school. Martin is talking about going back to school!"

"Oh, don't be ridiculous; any more of that talk and I'll tell the doctor to put you in a ward full of children with a dragon of a nurse who doesn't know how to put a catheter in properly – believe me there are plenty of them around!"

Martin smiled. "It's okay, Mom – just talking. I'll take a few days off. Is that okay with you?"

His mother nodded.

There was a long silence and then when his mother had finally kissed him goodnight and closed the door, Martin said:

"I'm going back soon. I have to."

Dominika shook her head from side to side, but didn't say anything.

Later that night, when everyone was asleep, Martin was awakened by Magnus. Martin woke immediately, feeling surprisingly quite clear headed and refreshed.

What Magnus had in his mouth surprised him even more: it was one of his father's slippers. Where on earth had he found it? he wondered.

Martin knew, without a moment's hesitation that his father, or, rather, Ish-chaer was calling him. He felt the side of his head, shook it a little and lay back again on his pillow. Would there be something in Tantalis, perhaps something Queen Fara could give him to heal the wound? Would the key give him enough strength? Did the elves have some secret, or the faeries some potion or medicine that could make sure he would feel better? He didn't want to risk his life and health – the blow had been serious, and he couldn't simply ignore what the doctor had said.

But perhaps now that Ish-chaer was calling him, things were better. Perhaps they even knew what had happened to him, and that's why he was calling him back.

Martin made up his mind.

He put on the clothes that lay on his bed; and patted the mattress next to him, beckoning Magnus to jump up. He put his arm around his dog's neck, finally ready.

There was no way he could climb over Dominika and get into his wheelchair. Besides he knew that he had the confidence and ability to get into Tantalis without using the old oak as a portal. All he needed was the key.

But then he suddenly realised he didn't have the key! How would he return? He panicked and felt a cold wave rush over him again.

Then he remembered Morduainé's words – *you are the key.*

Holding Magnus tightly, he closed his eyes and said the Latin inscription softly without any hesitation.

It was immediate.

But this time it was neither a soft landing nor an appropriate one. Martin had expected to land at the Console in the room where Edytya found him, or at some tree in the Dark Woods.

But it was to be – oh, no; that would have been far too easy.

Immediately, Martin began to regret his hasty decision

because when he looked around he realised they were in the wrong place.

And very much at the wrong time.

::: eighteen :::
The Turning Point

in medias res
into the midst of things

Ish-chaer stood next to Morduainé.

"Are you sure you've come out at the right time?"

"Only time will tell, Morduainé; it is certainly good to be at your side again. It's been quite a journey I've made. When last did we stand together?"

Morduainé got off his tricorn – Diablo and the Inkwas were now far away, regrouping or perhaps even retreating – they would have to make a decision about what their next move should be.

Ish-chaer looked at him pensively, brushing his long white hair away from his face. "The years escape me – perhaps more than five hundred – I was an Inkwa for two hundred or so re-member."

The two of them stood and looked out over the plain now, both trying to regain some perspective. Memories. Each one was aware of the journey they had made and the point to which they had now come, and their expressions reflected their pensive mood.

"What do you think their next move will be?" Ish-chaer

asked, finally.

Morduainé spoke while he stroked the long hair on the neck of his tricorn, not taking his eyes off the enemy for a second:

"I was sad to see the degree of Diablo's temper and resolve; he is no longer just a troublesome Inkwa, but turned fully to embody as much evil as possible. I can now understand how the killing of two dragones came about. Unless they turn to attack again, I think Phantoam and the other dragones should try to drive them back fully. We cannot have any kind of soppy retreat – this must be a decisive battle. There is too much at stake."

Ish-chaer nodded, showing for the first time a sadness in his eyes.

"But I am not certain of the wisdom of your appearance here," observed Morduainé.

"I don't think I could have stayed protected where I was any longer. If Diablo is killing dragones, who's to say they will ignore no-place-land and respect it – there, I was all alone without any protection. At least here I have all of you. I am finally back home. It is where I need to be right now; I am sure of it."

Morduainé nodded, allowing a slight smile. They were silent for a long while, and then Ish-chaer noticed something:

"What's that?"

233

"What?" said Morduainé, following Ish-chaer's gaze.

"Over there in the middle of the field. It's ... it can't be. Someone has appeared in the middle of the plain, right between us and the Inkwas. Look – it looks like a human dog! By the magic of all the faeries and the songs of the trolls, it's Martin and Magnus his dog! How on earth!?"

"This is not good; he was told to wait."

"I said I would call him, but I have not focussed my attention towards him at all; if anything I have pushed him away. Why didn't he listen?"

"Someone had better reach him quickly," said Morduainé.

"That can only be me," said Ish-chaer.

"I don't think that's wise. We cannot have the two most important people in Tantalis in the middle of the plains. What if Diablo turns around and sees both of you?"

But Ish-chaer did not stay to debate with his friend and confidant, Morduainé. Instead he gripped his sword and bow and ran as fast as he could towards both Martin and Magnus.

He was not the only one who had seen him. When Martin looked up the slight slope of the hill to his left, he realised he might be in trouble.

It was Diablo.

He had also seen Martin, and was already turning to run

234

down the slope towards him.

Magnus could sense the danger and ran towards him, barking frantically. Martin tried to call him back, realising that he was no match for this huge creature coming down the hill. But it was no use.

Diablo was by now almost in full flight. He galloped, his tail giving him added momentum as he leant back onto it every now and then, the rippling muscles in his huge legs pumping as hard as they could to launch himself forward each time his feet landed on the ground. He began to scream, his red flicking tongue adding to his fearsome appearance.

From the opposite side came Ish-chaer running only as an elf in full flight could run: his head down, bent forward, hair flowing behind him, and increasing his speed with each step until he looked as though he was as light as air and running as fast as a puckish wind.

Martin was in the middle.

He realised that it would take another few seconds for Diablo to reach him. Would Ish-chaer make it in time? What if Diablo was able to throw something at him – a sword or spear, for instance? Martin's mind was in overdrive, frantic, and once again his head began to throb.

And then as he found himself stepping backwards towards

Ish-chaer and away from the frightening creature coming down the slope, he stumbled on something.

He looked down. It was an Inkwa spear.

Instinctively he picked it up, holding it in his right hand. He looked at Diablo, coming nearer each moment and then, turning his head, at Ish-chaer. He realised he would not make it in time. There was no mistaking Diablo's intentions. Martin knew instinctively there would be no capture, no talk – it would be a quick and decisive death.

Martin didn't want to die.

He found himself holding the spear as he would a javelin. A javelin! Martin suddenly realised what he had in his hand. Could he do it? He looked back once again. Ish-chaer was nearer, approaching with every second; but not quite near enough.

And Diablo …

Martin could feel his heart exploding inside his chest; so much so he could hardly breathe. The thought of Diablo reaching him first; surely his father had not called him back to die, surely this was not what Tantalis wanted!

He tightened his grip on the long spear. It was beautifully balanced and fitted perfectly into his hand. He allowed it to bounce once or twice, up and down. Could he do it?

He shook his head, his heart pounding, racing, and then with one quick action his arm fell behind and below him. For just a split second before the launch, Martin had a moment of doubt – he was not in his chair now, and launching a javelin while standing up was quite a different action.

Suddenly he found himself screaming loudly: "Whaaaaa!"

Instinctively, his arm came up and forward, the spearhead almost touching the side of his face. And when he threw it, he could just about see the red of Diablo's tongue, and the fire in his eyes; his tail-end swaying behind his massive body as his feet pounded the ground beneath him.

It was what Diablo least expected. When he finally realised what was happening, his momentum was too quick and his direction too committed. It was simply too late to stop, and he could no more sidestep the spear than redirect its path.

Martin could actually see the look of surprise on Diablo's face as the spear itself reached him and found its mark.

It took him at full force, just below the chest, and on the right side of his abdomen, near his heart. His two hands immediately grabbed hold of the shaft, as his body continued on its now futile path. His legs began to falter, though, and no longer did the landing of his feet on the ground produce their rhythmical beat. They landed sporadically; and then one foot simply didn't make it at all.

When Diablo fell, he did so on his side, only four or five metres from Martin and with a gigantic thud.

Martin could see, for just a second, a look of contempt for him, but also one of pain and marked surprise.

Martin felt almost sorry for him.

Magnus barked frantically, at and around Diablo's face.

Martin suddenly realised he had been holding his breath all the time; and when he let out a blast of air he had to hold on to his chest, pounding it again and again in an attempt to stop his heart from exploding inside him.

Ish-chaer reached him, perhaps a second or two later.

"Thank Heaven itself you're alright." He looked down at Diablo. "Have you killed him?" he asked turning again to Martin.

Martin was still in a state of shock; all he could do was stare at the awesome creature on the ground. Ish-chaer took hold of him and, drawing Martin to one side, he stepped forward in a slow deliberate approach to inspect Diablo. He was still moving slightly, shuddering every now and then.

Suddenly there was the sound of more feet behind Martin, and he turned to see Trollip, and two other trolls with him.

"Stand back," said Trollip. "OoOoooo-ee; Yes! If he not dead, I kill him, for you." His sword was already above his head.

And he brought it down fast and furiously.

With one swift blow it was the end.

The other two trolls gathered around Martin, their mouths slightly open. They simply could not take their eyes off him – little did Martin realise that he had done something few in Tantalis might have had the courage or ability to do.

Ish-chaer turned to Martin. "I don't think we should stay here – look!" He pointed up the slight slope. Some of the Inkwas, seeing what had happened began to run down towards them; a few beginning to bellow and scream, as they gained momentum. They must have realised their leader was down; perhaps they wanted to rescue him.

Almost certainly they would want revenge.

It was a good time to retreat. Ish-chaer tapped Trollip on the shoulder, indicating that they should follow.

Martin and Ish-chaer began to run. Soon Martin realised the trolls had caught up with them, but he was no match for either Ish-chaer, whose elfin speed and grace clearly surpassed that of humans, or for the trolls who also managed, with their strange running gait and not entirely unlike that of an Inkwa, to run much faster than Martin could imagine any human doing.

He fell behind. Now and then Ish-chaer slowed and turned in order to encourage him to catch up, but he simply could not.

The Inkwas were gaining ground, and Martin was not even half way back to the elfin ranks. Ahead of them in the distance he could see trolls fall to the ground, taking their typical battle stance in readiness for the torrent of Inkwas that would come their way.

The elves had knelt down, their arrows drawn. They would surely fire over his head, at the right moment, in order to catch the storming Inkwas as they approached behind Martin.

It did not matter what Ish-chaer said or did, it was no use. Martin simply could not run that fast; and it was clear that the Inkwas, if not all, at least some, would reach him before he managed to cross the plain to safety. He could feel a throbbing in his head, his heart wildly pounding inside his chest. He ran, and ran. His legs thrust out in front of him, then crashing into the ground, one over the other, again and again. And no matter how much he pushed them to work harder, it seemed he was still so very far away.

He began to panic. It was easy to recite inscriptions and hold on to keys when one was sitting quietly inside a tree – this was an entirely different matter!

The inscription! Yes, that was it! He started, *"stultum ...."* But only the first word came out. He could not concentrate – there was simply too much to distract him. He felt his heart thrashing inside his chest, his feet hardly touching the ground. One wrong step; just *one* bad landing.

Then it happened.

Wham! He could feel the front of his left foot smash into a mound of earth. His body bent forward, instinctively, in order to correct his balance. For a second he looked like a runner eager to reach the tape of the finish-line first – his head bent forward, his body arched. But this was no finish of a champion runner – it didn't take long and he landed face first in the grass. Martin could feel the soft earth graze against his face, his hands and arms coming up instantly to protect himself. He was down, flat on the ground. And there was absolutely no chance of getting up and resuming his flight.

Ish-chaer had not noticed, and continued speeding forward.

For a second or two there was silence. All that Martin could do was feel, against the side of his face, the erratic thudding of large Inkwish feet hitting the ground not too far behind him. The thudding grew, even in the short space of time he lay face down, louder and louder.

There was clearly no way he was going to be able to get up and make it to the other side. Magnus barked frantically at his head, desperate for his master to rise perhaps even remembering the last time he lay on the ground, cold and lifeless.

Perhaps he finished the inscription right then, perhaps he did not. He would never remember. But louder than the thudding of Inkwish feet was the sound of something thunderous directly above him.

It was an almost deafening swish, and it reminded him of the sound of a helicopter. It was somehow gentler and far less mechanical in nature. Nevertheless Martin had the impression that it was something very large.

It was as if time stood still – pictures of rescue helicopters came to mind; then it was images of Inkwas towering above him.

Martin was beginning to waft again – perhaps the fall had injured him further, knocking him a little senseless and bringing on further concussion. Was he drifting away somewhere? Was he perhaps entering a portal? He couldn't tell. And just when he felt himself beginning to lose focus, he opened his eyes and recognised the creature above him. A creature so large, that the sunlight was dimmed, and a shadow began to fall on the ground all around him.

It was neither the sound of the Inkwish nor that of a helicopter. It was the clear, and undeniable sound of the largest dragone in Tantalis. It was Phantoam.

He landed with an enormous **thud**! not more than a few

metres away from Martin. Martin tried to get to his feet.

"Don't lie there staring at me," he said. "You've got perhaps another ten seconds. Get up and jump on!"

Martin got up, a little dazed, his legs somewhat wobbly and weak. He scrambled towards Phantoam. Out of the corner of his eye he could see that an Inkwa was uncomfortably close; his spear ready, drawn back, his speed slightly reduced so as to make the throw.

There was no more time. He jumped onto Phantoam's side, clutching his small wing, clinging frantically to any piece of him that protruded from his massive bulk, and climbed onto his back, just as Phantoam began to rise. He had always wondered whether the fin-like ridges on the back of a dragone were sharp, or hard – he was about to find out. He simply grabbed one and held on tightly.

Phantoam began to breath in and out frantically. Martin could sense a level of panic in him. Phantoam let out a blast of flame to discourage any Inkwa from getting too close and then, suddenly, they were floating upwards. They rose quickly, and the action seemed to demand much from Phantoam himself.

Martin could sense, too, that this was perhaps much quicker than a dragone's normal ascent. They were high above the battleground now, and something was going on inside the gargantuan body right beneath Martin.

"What's that noise?" he shouted. At first Phantoam did not reply. He was still breathing in and out heavily, panting, and at the same time making strange sounds with his stomach.

"I have to make enough gas as quickly as possible to rise in the air," he shouted back. "And if we don't get high enough they will be able to aim their spears at my underbelly. And that will be the end of us! Hold on!"

Soon they were more than high enough to be out of reach. But Inkwas swirled below them, seething with rage, erupting with avid determination. Martin peered over the side, leaning as far as he dared without falling off Phantoam's back.

"What were you doing down there in the middle of all that chaos?" asked Phantoam when he had gathered his breath.

"I don't know," said Martin, trying to gather himself. "Something must be wrong with the portals, I've never had trouble coming into or leaving Tantalis before."

"Well, you're lucky I saw you when I did."

Martin could actually hear the swish of the Inkwa's spears flying swiftly just under them. But Phantoam was too high; the spears lost their momentum, and began falling to the ground.

In frustration some Inkwas ran towards Magnus and kicked him so that he yelped loudly and rolled across into a tuft of grass. One managed to launch its tail-end and slice Magnus's leg wide open. Magnus cried out again, so loudly that Martin could hear him. Martin himself cried out from above, desperate, but unable to do anything.

Phantoam hovered just above the crowding Inkwas, allowing Martin a perfect bird's eye view. Some Inkwas were gathering to look at Diablo, others continued to run. Most of them milled around below Phantoam, as though they thought they might have a chance at combat. It was chaotic, and probably what the elves were waiting for.

Their arrows, straight and accurate, caught the faltering Inkwas below; they floundered this way and that, not using their shields effectively. Many of them fell, at their leader's side.

The rest of them, still running, seemed to lose direction and began to scatter.

The trolls were waiting for them, but instead of waiting until the last moment, they rose from their positions between the long grass and ran to meet the rush of disorganised Inkwas.

The clash was almighty: the sound itself and the force of bodies and steel colliding with such violence. The trolls, diminutive, and seemingly no match for the tall and heavy Inkwas, fought with such determination, they soon began to unravel any fighting strength or resolve in their much larger enemy.

245

Within seconds rows of Inkwas lay, their blood spilling into the Soft Plains, and forming small rivers that made patterns on some patches of dry earth.

Martin thought about Magnus. He closed his eyes – it was almost over. Phantoam brought them lower now, obviously feeling it was safer.

Faeries rushed in, some to stare at Diablo, others to rescue Magnus: one rubbed a mixture of earth and something she took out of a small bag into his wound, and Magnus raised his head from his pillow of soft grass and gazed at them. Martin smiled, relieved, from high above.

"Come," said Phantoam after some time. "We must muster the remaining Inkwas – whatever Morduainé decides to do, we must gather the rest of them here on the open plain. Hold on."

And they flew.

Martin realised, probably for the first time, that he was actually flying on a dragone's back. The excitement and panic of climbing onto Phantoam, and then rising up into the air as fast as they could had not really allowed this to sink in. Now they were flying, not fast, but definitely moving. And it was a strange sensation. He had flown before, often, in fact. But flight with man always meant noise. Up here it was silent – a hushed, heavy, but somewhat comforting silence.

They swept across the now empty plain, Phantoam making a deep sighing sound, not unlike the slow, long song of a whale – indeed he was about the same size, and summoned the other dragones to follow him. Soon the sky was thick with their mass, the small intermittent flap of their wings, which they used only for manoeuvring, and the rising and falling of their bloated bodies.

The Inkwas, mostly stunned by what they had witnessed, were now completely scattered – some running away, some quite motionless in position where Diablo had left them.

The dragones positioned themselves on the other side, behind them so as to drive them, like cattle, towards the main body of elves, trolls and faeries.

And then the final onslaught began.

The dragones swept down, onto the seething mass of Inkwas, now desperate in their attempt to get away, and with their fiery breath, unleashed a fury of flame above their heads, catching them on their necks and shoulders.

The Inkwas ran, galloped, fell crashing to the ground; some got up again to run further – anything, just to get away; and all the time they were being herded towards the main body of their enemy.

Over the small hill, back onto the plain, they ran so that from above, it looked like a swarm of rats running to a sure and fatal end.

"Stop!" said Martin to Phantoam. "Please put me down."

"I don't think that's a good idea," said Phantoam.

"Please – you must. Right next to Morduainé. I must speak with him."

The remaining Inkwas were now where they had been in the first place, although not at all in their former glory, and not assembled in their tight formations, but instead quivering, looking this way and that.

The faeries positioned themselves again – this would be another chance for them, especially with the Inkwas so disorganised. It would be an easy attack.

Phantoam landed and Martin climbed off; he walked to Morduainé who stood next to his tricorn.

"I must speak to them – I have something to say," Martin said.

Morduainé shook his head, more out of curiosity and indecision than anything else. "Speak with the Inkwas?"

"Yes. I know this is what I have to do. I just know it." He could hear Morduainé breathing – the air was heavy with heat and the soft whining of the Inkwas some distance away.

Martin climbed onto Phantoam's back and stood up, as tall as he could, so that he could see over Phantoam's head and directly into the eyes of the Inkwas now gathered in a long line abreast.

There was silence. Perhaps they were transfixed by Phantoam's presence, perhaps the sight of Martin had arrested them but few if any of them moved at all. Martin spoke.

"Inkwas. Your leader is dead. There is no escape now. They will open the Box and you'll no longer enjoy the power you had. I cannot guarantee the dragones will hold back, but for now, they hover above you all and you have our attention. Tantalis is not a place of death – this today should never have happened. There is even one of you that tried to kill me. Look," and Martin parted his hair to reveal his fresh wound on the side of his head.

"Queen Fara has told me that you have the choice to turn and become elves again in your former glorious state. Do it now, before it's too late!"

If ever silence had washed over the Soft Plains, it was now, like a soft lapping pond against a gentle shore, the silence, thick and pregnant, filled every being assembled there. Even the heavy breathing of Phantoam was arrested by Martin's words and his plea.

The Inkwas stared at Martin; one here, one there gripped their swords more firmly, another his shield, looking at one another, unsure.

It was another few agonising minutes before two Inkwas lowered their weapons and walked forward gingerly.

And then more, and more, until great gaps in their ranks formed. There must have been two or three thousand that slowly edged their way towards Martin and Phantoam.

Magnus lay at the tricorn's feet, his head raised, poised to growl, with three faeries hovering above him, the soft hum of their wings fanning him to keep him cool.

The elves began to cheer. And then the trolls. And then, even Jezze-B, lifting herself off the ground and raising her arms above her head, began to shout with joy.

The Inkwas walked on and on towards them, and then seemingly without fear, but with looks of utter defeat and resignation, stopped right in front of the cheering crowd.

No one had even contemplated this beckoning, a call of this nature, and even Morduainé was smiling. Perhaps, he thought, this is why they had needed a human-child to enter Tantalis – for this, if nothing else. He shook his head, almost not believing what was happening before his very eyes.

And then the most beautiful song rose from the ranks of

the elves. A haunting song of victory, of praise and honour – a hymn, a song of battle, a rousing chorus of triumph all rolled into one.

Martin stood laughing on Phantoam's back.

And then he could simply not help himself, so he raised his own arms and shouted for joy as well.

::: nineteen :::

The Return

pax vobiscum
peace be with you

The narrow passage through the hills must have groaned under the weight of all who marched through that day.

The trolls escorted the turned Inkwas – they were looking confused, but decidedly more at peace than after the herding by the dragones. They were at least certain of a better future, yet unsure of what was expected of them in order to get there.

It was a kind of psychological no-man's land for all of them.

The elves sang all the way and the faeries could not keep still or find it in themselves to walk with the others, so they buzzed overhead, flitting from one group to another, recounting their bravery and the overall victory. In general, they made a nuisance of themselves by suddenly descending to crack a joke, or ask a question, with 'don't you think ...', or 'remember when ...', or 'wasn't it amazing when ...'

Many of the Inkwas had had no contact with faeries for most of their lives and were puzzled, not quite sure how to deal with them; some were even frightened after their ordeal with the

Weeping Moth Plant, and each time a faery flew overhead, some fell to the ground with a whimper.

Martin flew with Phantoam, victorious.

It was amazing to see Tantalis from above, and when Phantoam rose high in the sky above the column of marchers below, he could even see the Dark Woods beyond.

"Where were the bad trolls in all of this?" he asked.

"Oh, they are nothing more than nuisance value; quite different from the trolls we know; they are generally frightened of conflict. You will probably find they're slinking about in the Dark Woods right now," said Phantoam.

"I still don't fully understand how you fly – I can see that you don't need your wings except to change direction; and you talk about gas in your stomach."

"That's it. That's what gives me lift."

"I can remember when we first met you said I was asking the wrong question."

"I do remember."

"I was wondering how something so big could fly with such small wings."

"That sounds very human to me," said Phantoam, chuckling. "What do you think you should have been asking, now that you know?"

253

"Well," thought Martin, sitting up and enjoying the view; the hills were becoming more convoluted and mountains began to appear, and he realised they were approaching Queen Fara's palace entrance and the settlements of the elves. It was so well camouflaged, he battled to recognise it, even from the air. "I suppose I should be asking, why do you need to be so big in order to fly?"

"Congratulations, you've got it! And what's the answer?"

"Because your stomach is full of gas?"

"Aha …!" said Phantoam so loudly that some of the other dragones turned to look at them both.

"Now you know my secret – there's not much more to me besides a lot of hot air!"

Martin laughed: "Is that where the expression came from?"

"Now be careful, young man, you might just be saying the wrong thing."

"Okay," said Martin, let's see if I can get this right, "you mix some chemical in your body with …. what?"

"I have hydrochloric acid in the stomach, just like you, and a mechanism to draw masses of calcium from my bones. If you pay attention in science class, you'll be able to work out that a reaction between the two makes a perfect gas – hydrogen – it's much lighter than air; and so up, up we go!"

And with that Phantoam's stomach rumbled and they rose even higher, making the hills below look like small mounds.

Now Martin had to shout; it was getting cold and there was some wind also.

"So the excess gases when mixed with air, make the fiery breath?"

"Sounds like you've been paying attention in science class after all," shouted Phantoam.

"And," said Martin, "now I finally understand why your lair has to be covered in gold! It's the only metal that isn't eaten away by hydrochloric acid!"

"We'll make a new Atlantian scientist out of you yet!" said Phantoam, shooting out a long column of yellow and bright orange flames against the deep blue sky.

The other dragones, floating behind and in formation, did the same and far below they could only just make out the cheer of thousands of joyful elves, faeries and trolls.

When they returned to the palace Queen Fara was waiting for them.

There was de-mobbing to be done; cleaning up and the preparation of the one elf who had been killed – he would be buried in the mountain side at the Waterfall – at Dragone's Lair.

Martin placed Magnus in the courtyard, next to the table

and the fountain pool. There he lay, trying to get up whenever someone came to congratulate him on his bravery, but with strict instructions from Martin to lie back down.

Queen Fara announced a feast for the next day. Almost everyone in the settlements and beyond, except for the women, had been involved, and much had to be arranged – they would use the Great Hall so that the dragones could be honoured, and together they would plan the most important event in the history of Tantalis: the return to Dragone's Lair and the opening of the Box.

It was to be a reality finally, although everyone was unsure of the consequences, except that they would usher a new beginning into their own hearts and that of the human world. They bristled with anticipation and sheer excitement.

The elfin children, who were the chefs of Tantalis, scurried this way and that, with flowers, fruit, fish and vegetables, and some meat and a host of recipes – each one bringing something for Queen Fara, Morduainé and then Martin to sample, taste, or approve.

There would be Weeping Moth Plant stew, served with freshly painted potatoes, Phisteriss water-rat marinated in the juices of the Mountain Leopard Flowering Fern (which tasted like mild chilli sauce and tomatoes; the fern looking nothing like a

256

leopard). Elfin beans (they looked like ears) soaked, and which tasted like bitter-sweet chocolate when soaked overnight in fresh dew from the mountains. Mountain Rock Fern stalks (a little like asparagus), soaked in lime cream, deep fried in batter and served with a Troll Sword sauce (this had a sharp edge to it).

But the greatest delicacy of all, loved by both elves and faeries but not particularly by the trolls, was Frog Omelette – this was a special dish because it was the privilege of faery children below the age of eleven to collect, from the burial grounds of frogs, their eye-balls and stomachs (remember that elves did not kill anything, and so this meant that burial grounds had to be found, where, once a quarter, aged frogs in their masses went to die).

Once prayers were uttered by the faery children in a special rite, they removed the eyes and stomachs and marinated these overnight in a herb not unlike lavender. Then they collected eggs from the Phisteriss water-rat, and once the omelette was made, and just before serving, folded the frog remains into the omelette itself with just a sprinkling of cheese. It was a starter that Queen Fara was especially fond of. Of course, only elfin children above twelve did the actual cooking.

The list was endless.

The faery children were insistent that they explain everything to Martin himself, and sometimes got the details wrong, incurring the chagrin of the elfin children, who made sure they were immediately corrected.

There was a huge ellöe-cloêsh (directly translated from Elfin, as a *hullabaloo*) when one of the children entered the courtyard to announce that Mountain Rock Fern stalks were in short supply – apparently this was the favourite vegetable of the dragones and there would not be nearly enough. Some weary trolls were immediately dispatched to search for those less visible against the hillside.

Martin found that he was exhausted, and could do little more than sit on his enormous woollen cushion at the table, next to Magnus, and watch the frantic activity reflected in the carvings on the table itself. Each time something significant happened, like a troll finding a new fern, some faeries rushed to the table to see where he had found it and applauded with great gusto.

The other trolls who were in charge of wine-making constantly fought with Jezze-B and other faeries who were assigned the task of bottling (wine was only bottled immediately before use), and the choice of specific wines for each course.

The only regret of the day was the discovery that neither Armai nor Geaddon were amongst the turned Inkwas, nor were their bodies found amongst their dead.

258

Queen Fara shook her head. "This is not very good news," she said, "we think that the opening of the Box, according to Ish-chaer, only unleashes the potential and opportunity for the rest of the Inkwas to turn; this means they can refuse and cause more trouble in the future."

"Does that mean the Essence doesn't work?" asked Martin.

"Well, you must realise that we don't know exactly what it will do, except we do know it unleashes the potential itself – it will fully restore those Inkwas who have turned, back into elves like us, strengthening our numbers and making our collective spirit that much stronger.

And we do also know that Tantalis' spirit will be re-united with humans in the form of Atlantis. I think that is enough for us – going back to a world I can remember as a child will be quite enough for me, and will give us opportunities of controlling those who have not turned. Still, it would have been better for all if the two of them had joined the rest."

Martin was determined not to let this news spoil his day.

"What made you address them as you did?" asked Fara eventually, sitting down opposite him.

"There was something in their eyes, I think. I cannot explain it, but I almost felt sorry for them, as though they were trapped. I guess I know what it's like to be offered a second chance."

Fara smiled at him, and Martin felt a warm glow, as though renewed strength was suddenly flowing from his head to his toes.

The next day, around mid-morning (morning meals were the focus of the day in Tantalis) they all gathered in the Great Hall.

The spread was awe-inspiring and took Martin's breath away as he tried to take in the colours, textures and sheer volume of food on the heavily laden tables. Each table itself had a carved troll or faery as its leg, but this was no ordinary carving, of course – the faeries not only spoke as one passed, but sometimes even pinched Martin on his bum. It took him some time to work out what was happening, and it was only when he heard a giggle coming from the table-leg itself that he saw the sudden movement of a faery returning to her original position.

He shook his head – this place is crazy! he thought to himself, and then just hoped that they had placed him at a table without any naughty faeries or trolls to distract him from his meal.

In the middle of each table was a bowl of flowers and herbs; they had obviously been carefully chosen in that they all seemed to belong to one another. When Martin stood staring at one of the bowls he was amazed to see two of the herbs, one very much like rosemary and another that looked altogether strange, rub themselves against the stalk of a flower – the flower then turned with a circular movement, a little like a belly dancer.

Another bushy herb had a small insect hiding amongst its leaves. It seemed to be playing a game with a tall lily; it would reach out and tickle the stem of the lily which would vibrate quite violently – this all seemed to be a game, with the insect scurrying back and forth from inside the leaves of the herb.

Martin was almost sure he heard the insect laugh. Or was it the lily?

All seemed to be ready and they finally sat down.

He expected a great number of speeches and formal announcements, as adults so often make at occasions like these, but there were none – it seemed, after talking to Jezze-B who had placed herself next to him, that in Tantalis, eating was far too much fun for that kind of thing. They would do that later.

Martin suddenly thought of something and made his way across the hall to talk to Phantoam. He was busy eating a huge helping of something the smelled of mild curry.

"I was thinking," said Martin, when he finally got Phantoam's attention. "Queen Fara says we're going to bury the elf that was killed, outside Dragone's lair. What happened to the dragones that were killed – did you bury them?"

Phantoam shifted his great body to make himself more comfortable, and turning his head a little this way and that, brought it right down so that Martin could smell the characteristic forest-like smell of a dragone on his breath. "We don't bury dragones," said Phantoam.

Martin was a little afraid he might have insulted Phantoam so instead of reacting, he decided to keep quiet.

"You're wondering what happens to them, aren't you?" said Phantoam.

Martin nodded. "They must go somewhere," he eventually said.

"Why do you think humans have never been able to 'prove' the existence of dragons. What about fossil remains?" Phantoam drew back again, leaving Martin to his own devises.

This was definitely a challenge, and Martin knew that Phantoam would be disappointed in him if he could not work it out. He helped himself to a large piece of pie that dripped with a sticky, deep red substance and that smelled like cinnamon and berries, and took a bite. It was just divine; there were berries inside and they began to jump around in his mouth, exploding like little cannon balls and making the pie itself even more delicious. When he had managed to catch them all inside his mouth and swallow, he finally said:

"They obviously disappear."

"Aha!" said Phantoam. "You're absolutely right – they disappear, but for a practical reason – no secret or 'mythical' hiding place or burial ground. They disappear entirely. Can you think why?"

Martin took another bite, and thought hard: they disappear, poof! Into thin air? They're buried deep in water, caves? No, can't be because then humans would have unearthed them at some time. Martin scratched his head.

Why had his father never taken him to a dragon dig? Suddenly his mind was in overdrive. Yes, that was a really good question - why *hadn't* his father taken him to a dragon dig? He was trying to think of a time when his father might have spoken about dragons. Martin shook his head; he couldn't remember him ever having done so. No. He had never taken him to a dragon dig because there weren't any!

Martin knew that dragones had separated themselves, with all other 'mythical' creatures from the human world. True. But they would not have been able to extract all dragone remains also, surely.

"I'll leave you to your thoughts," said Phantoam, "while I continue with this delightful meal!" He began to chuckle as a faery tickled him with a large leafy herb.

Martin took another bite of the pie and while the berries continued to tickle his own mouth with their tiny explosions, he imagined a dragon dig – he pictured the bones, the neck and head, just as he had once seen the fossil remains of a dinosaur buried neatly in the ground. No remains. Why not? There was the ground in front of him – he could see the dinosaur; but no dragon, or dragone. No, the ground was empty: no bones, no fossil remains. He just shook his head. "I give up!"

"Give up! You! Of all people I know, *give up*." Phantoam laughed out aloud. And then suddenly he looked serious: "Think of the essence." Phantoam peered down at Martin, cocking his head to one side so that he could peer at him from one eye only. "Think of what's *inside*!" he said.

This time it didn't take Martin long.

"I've got it," he said suddenly, with some berries popping out of this mouth. "Their essence; the … the hydrochloric acid … it eats them up! And so there's nothing left to be fossilized."

"Horaah! I knew you'd get it," said Phantoam, this time flapping his tiny wings. "There's nothing to bury. Of course! The skin and internal organs simply dry up – *they* might remain, but not for long. The bones themselves disappear. No bones, no re-mains. So you see, that's why there's nothing to bury, and no fossil remains!"

The faery tending to Phantoam suddenly burst out in hysterical laughter. "Nothing to bury!" She laughed and laughed. "It's so funny – bury. What do you want to bury?" she spluttered in between her laughter.

"You'll have to forgive her – we haven't had to bury anything for eons; I am sure there are many here who don't even know what it means!" said Phantoam. "Besides, I'm sure she's had far too much to drink," he said, winking at Martin.

Soon faeries and trolls all around were laughing, with some trolls feigning a burial as they lay on the ground; but they were unable to keep still and rolled over with laughter while faeries tickled them from above.

Everyone ate and laughed, faeries told jokes about trolls, the trolls then told jokes at the elves expense, and this while everyone enjoyed each morsel of food to the maximum. The only sign of anything formal was when someone stood up and said something complimentary about a dish. One of the children who had cooked it would then come forward, in the form of a hologram, and take a bow while everyone cheered.

The other dragones were also in the centre, themselves eating, with faeries feeding them copious amounts of their favourite foods. Even this was a game, and the faeries would make them close their eyes and guess what it was they were serving them, and then laugh wildly if any dragone got it wrong.

The meal finally came to an end.

They were all exhausted, and some even curled up on the ground next to their tables, to sleep the meal off.

Martin returned to the courtyard with Queen Fara, Trollip and Jezze-B, and there found his own cushion. It was a little more than a minute before his eyes were shut and he was fast asleep, and he was dreaming of fossils, dragones and laughing faeries.

::: twenty :::
The Final Journey

non est alter
there is no other

It began early the next morning, and it was as if they were again going to war. Except this time, although there were long columns of elves and trolls, and faeries buzzing above, there were no weapons. And instead of the sound of a war-cry or the sound of spears and arrows making their way through the air, there was the sound of everyone singing with renewed joy.

The turned Inkwas, still looking much like Inkwas, but somewhat changed in appearance now, looked a little happier with themselves. They were in an expectant mood, and it was this that made them look different, perhaps.

It was decided to leave Magnus behind, with a faery in attendance – Magnus was not impressed. Martin rode, this time, on Emmazelle, the tricorn from the courtyard with his first visit, and next to Morduainè.

And Queen Fara, for the first time since the trouble started, was about to venture beyond her own palace. Martin could sense great anticipation in the air and that this journey was probably the most important the citizens of Tantalis had ever made.

They exited the palace settlements from a different side, but also through a very narrow passage, one almost as narrow as that which Martin and Dominika had entered the very first time. The rock face rose high on both sides, allowing in only limited light, and when they broke through on the other side to look out across a great valley the light bathed them with a blinding force that too their breath away. Martin battled to focus for some time and then when he could he realised someone was right next to him. He scratched an itch on his forehead, and brushed the short fringe from his eyebrows so he could get a better view of who it was. It was Jezze-b

"You've settled down nicely in Tantalis," she said, hovering next to Emmazelle's head; the tricorn turned to look at Jezze-b and gave a short snort of recognition, her head bobbing up and down slightly. "I was really uncertain about you the first time we met. Are you going to stay?"

"Stay?" asked Martin. Emmazelle turned her head around to look at Martin, as if expecting an answer.

"Yeah, I mean right here in Tantalis." Jezze-B hesitated and then added, "It's gotta be much better than living with humans; I can't imagine why you would want to go back," she said with a smirk.

268

"Well, I don't think I have much of a choice really; besides it sounds as if I'm some kind of link between the human world and Atlantis. It looks like I'll have to go back."

Jezze-B was stunned. She stopped flitting about in the air and remained motionless, so that she seemed to drift past them as Emmazelle and Martin continued on their journey. "So ... you mean you know?!"

"Know what?" asked Martin. She hurried forward, her wings buzzing wildly, and came right up to Martin's face. "You know about Tantalis – about Atlantis?"

Martin nodded and smiled broadly. There was silence for some time. Finally she said:

"You will return from time to time, won't you?" She was less surprised and seemed to have calmed down. Martin looked sideways at her, noticing for the first time her small curly nose and blushing-pink cheeks.

"If I don't will you miss me?" Martin smiled when he said this, remembering how impatient Jezze-B had been when they had met. She was clearly a little embarrassed and after looking back at Martin, with a face flush with nothingness to say yet with just a hint of a smile, she flew away to talk to someone else. Martin laughed.

For some of the time Trollip also joined Martin and sang

songs to him about the brave deeds of legendary trolls, and then also legends about the human world that sounded very strange.

One of the songs was about an air-ship called the Hindenburg – humans had stolen the secret of their flight from dragones and had tried to use the technology. But when they tried to fly it, the air-ship crashed, killing many people. As Trollip sang the song he added sounds and flailing arms and legs to dramatize the horror of the crash itself. Martin remembered his chat with Phantoam about flight and, while listening to the song, remembered something he had once seen on television. He could vaguely remember some of the details which they seemed to fit Trollip's story.

Later that afternoon they came to a plateau and Martin could hear the clear sound of thunderous water. Behind him the turned Inkwas looked decidedly uncomfortable and glanced at each other nervously. They huddled together, somehow forgetting their new-found energy and purpose and in a strange way began to look a little more like Inkwas than new elves; their apprehension and fear was almost tangible.

Some of the elves, and quite a few faeries herded them gently, talking and encouraging them. Clearly there was nothing to be afraid of.

Down the one side of the mountain they meandered; it

was not too steep, but just steep enough to make their passage a slow one, and with every step they had to be mindful of loose rocks and stones that could easily give way and cause them to fall. Emmazelle trod carefully but confidently, as though she had made this journey before. All the time the spray of the enormous waterfall peppered them with stinging drops of water, making them cool and drip as though their bodies were sweating on a humid day.

When they reached the bottom they were all able to gather beside the pool that stretched far into the distance – the water was jet black and, at the base of the waterfall, white-tricorns pranced about frantically. They bucked and boiled with such might, and with such an audible bellow that it was almost deafening. Martin imagined he could actually see tricorns galloping towards him out of the depths of the pond below itself: here they came, throwing their head up high, straining to be loosened – held back by some cruel master and yet wanting to be unleashed so they may gallop and play across the great expanse of the water itself and beyond.

They foamed and fumed in frothy anger, from one side to the other where the fall met with the pond, and their eagerness to be set free went so deep, Martin could see the white all the way to the bottom where rocks glistening with a million shards of light.

Almost every human had been to a place like this, thought Martin; on some special holiday, some camping trip, everyone had seen nature's power and majesty like this. He, probably more than most. But not anything he had seen had ever looked quite like Dragone's Pond.

The Inkwas were ordered in.

But it was not going to be a simple task. Ish-chaer joined Martin on a rock at the side of the pool and explained what was going to happen.

"While some of the trolls bury Leethrå, the elf that was killed, we need the turned Inkwas to cleanse themselves by jumping into the pond. Even though they've turned, they still have an inherent fear of water. It's not going to be easy."

Martin looked up at him. Although they had spoken often, he found it still difficult to get used to the idea that somewhere deep inside this regal looking elf, was his father.

"Why do they need to be cleansed?" he asked.

"It's like a baptism; it's both symbolic and also necessary as the water passes over Dragone's Lair, and because the Lair is the central energy point of Tantalis – the point from which the Power of Now and the Essence emanates, it carries great energy and healing. Of course it eventually reaches us – you're looking here at the water that will end up in the palace courtyard."

"I'm not sure about this," said Martin. "They just don't look as if they'll ever get into that water."

"It does look like they're having some trouble," said Ishchaer, with a little smile on his face. They have a natural fear of water in their Inkwa state. It makes the swim another means of transition."

"Can I go in?" asked Martin after they had stood looking at the self-conscious and fearful group for some time.

"Of course," said the tall, gentle being, once his father, and now once again an important and revered elf.

Martin unconsciously found himself taking off his clothes, and with one look at a group of Inkwas next to him, he dived straight into the pond. This was his favourite medium and, a powerful swimmer back home, he was overjoyed at being able to use his legs in the water once again. He found himself being caught up in the fight of the white-tricorns, and felt their pull beneath him. It was glorious and he dived, surfaced, and dived again with the sheer pleasure and thrill of feeling the rush and urgency of the clean water flow over him, washing his entire body.

When he surfaced, all the elves clapped in unison. Then they began to sing a song with a beautiful harmony that went on for a long time. All the time their gentle clapping continued to the beat of the song itself and was itself enticing. It was mesmerizing.

Then one Inkwa jumped. And then another … and another. When all of them finally surfaced from beneath the water, there was simple spontaneous applause in an attitude of celebration, from everyone on the shore.

And then reverent silence as though everyone had adopted an attitude of prayer. One by one the Inkwas got out of the water, each one greeted by a troll who led them away.

They were quite changed; now looking something like the transformation Martin had seen from the Inkwa to his father. They still had some Inkwa features, but it was as though a sculptor had started a marble statue and had not quite finished it, so the figures struggled to burst out of the marble, and into the world – Martin could remember so many of Michelangelo's unfinished Pieta's his father had shown him in Rome and Florence when they had visited there.

Ish-chaer was at the side of the pond to help Martin out. It was time to go further and enter the Lair itself.

The path rose gently on the right side of the pond, hugging the cliff-face until suddenly, behind the torrent and the spray, Martin realised he was looking at an opening. He was eager to get out of the fine mist and he shook his head so the drops of water flew off his matted hair and onto the ground of the cave, although he was still quite wet from the swim itself.

The Lair was almost as large as the Great Hall.

Peculiar shapes and gnarled formations in the rock and outcrops of many different colours, shades and textures made it look quite other-worldly. There was a strange, but somewhat familiar, red and orange tinge that threaded itself through the rock formations. In fact, when Martin held his head to one side, he realised that he was looking at a straight line of rock, but titled at a rather precarious angle. Was it a type of lichen, or some organic ore deep within the rock itself? Martin didn't know. He suddenly realised that had he stood beside his father, he might have asked him. He was suddenly very sad for the first time since discovering Tantalis. Or was it Atlantis?

Clearly, as he could remember from excursions with his father, these rocks had had some violent force erupt from beneath them and push them over onto their side.

They walked some distance into the bowels of the cave itself, until the roof opened up at the top. This was obviously how the original Dragone himself had entered, and how the dragones would enter now.

In fact only Phantoam himself joined them. He came down this time, a little more majestically than that fateful day in the Great Hall. Perhaps this holy place and the power within it managed to guide him more accurately.

His descent and landing was almost perfect.

They stood quite still.

There was silence.

Morduainè held the key in his hand.

Martin found himself beside his father-elf. It was the strangest feeling – no longer was this man his father, yet Martin could feel the tug of his own history. How could he not imagine that here they were again at some dig, some famous, intriguing, fascinating ancient place – his father about to make a new discovery?

He wanted to reach out and touch him, but simply could not bring himself to do so. When he looked at him, he realised how true it was. The memories were perhaps there, but this elf was not human and this being was not his father. Martin realised, perhaps, that he had made this journey also to finally bury the man he loved so much: to finally bury the man that had been his father.

Just then Ish-chaer turned towards him. He was not smiling but the look on his face made Martin realise he was not alone in his sadness. Was this the father-figure deep within Ish-chaer reaching out to him; identifying with him? Martin simply stared.

Queen Fara walked to the front. She looked at Phantoam as though waiting for something. When she was happy it was the right moment, she nodded.

Suddenly there was a great roar and the flames from his mouth curled through the air like wild locks of hair in a strong wind. Again.

And then against the side of the cave a curtain or veil of some kind disintegrated, revealing an altar made of stone. On it was the Box, exactly as Martin could remember it. Ish-chaer shifted his body, ostensibly in recognition also. Martin glanced sideways.

Morduainè handed the key to Ish-chaer. Martin looked out of the corner of his eye at the now familiar key that had drawn him so deep into this strange and wonderful world.

He missed it.

Quietly, Queen Fara began to chant:

"Or cheät pammatarro;

chëis summeitra leigh.

Deis Deum, spiritus parashinto ..."

The elves followed suit, and chanted the song with her.
She then beckoned to Ish-chaer who stepped forward with the key and put it in the keyhole. It was only then that Martin realised there were three keyholes in all.

He returned to stand beside Martin and looked down at him: "Here. It is your turn. You must open the one on the right."

Martin hesitated, taking the key in his hand. The familiarity of it felt good. Delicate, yet strong and powerful.

"The one on the right?" asked Martin.

Ish-chaer nodded and for a brief moment Martin could detect, in the movement of his head and the look in his eyes, something else familiar.

He stepped forward with a smile on his face, clearly feeling as though he were in the presence of all those behind him willing him to do this. He placed the key into the keyhole and turned. It was a smooth and effortless click and, then, he sensed a little disappointment deep in his heart as though deep down he were saying, *was that it?*

He withdrew the key, feeling only a deep sense of purpose and accomplishment, knowing that it had been his own resolve, rather than the key, that had been the real inspiration. Morduainè had been right in saying it had been what lay inside Martin himself that had drawn him and given him the courage to finally reach this point.

It was Queen Fara's turn, and Martin handed the key to her.

She placed it in the middle keyhole.

What a difference it made when *she* turned it. She, herself, all but disappeared, and was bathed in strong iridescent light as the Box itself opened.

Like the spray from a blowhole in the ocean, the light shot upwards and filled every crevice and every shadow in the cave. Martin found himself rocking on the balls of his feet, and a great weight rose from his shoulders as though every care, every past regret and every present stress was suddenly and effortlessly swept away.

Queen Fara called out, as though first in fear, and then she spoke:

"We are joined again with the Power of Now; let this sweep away the human pain of loss and regret of the past, the desire for the future and what they cannot have. Let Dragone's Essence filter through all those present, to the four corners of our new Tantalis ... Our risen and restored Atlantis!"

"**Atlantis**. Gougamê **Atlantis**," called the elves, in their tongue.

"**Atlantis**. Elloueshei **Atlantis!**" sang out the faeries in an ancient faery language they sometimes used.

"All Gougamê **Atlantis!**" shouted the trolls and the turned Inkwas.

Martin found himself saying 'Atlantis' too, but it came out

slowly and faltering – he was so busy enjoying the roller-coaster ride of being bathed in this powerful light and energy that he didn't want to move or say anything right now that might stop it. It was awesome, and his body quivered with sheer delight and a deep sense of wonder, reverence and humility.

It was as though he *was* the light.

Each one of the Inkwas came forward, in groups of about fifty – their bodies filtered by the angled beams of light dancing against the dark background of the cave itself as they approached the opened Box. Martin strained to see each one disappear as they approached, and then reappear in the form of a new glorious elf.

For every one, at least one other elf came forward and embraced them, calling them by their new name. Perhaps it was the name they had held before. Perhaps those coming forward, thought Martin, were family and friends from their former lives. Whatever, it was a joyful experience and everyone in the cave began to clap once again.

Martin could not help himself, and although it was difficult to follow the rhythm, he just let go and clapped for the sheer fun of it.

Instinctively he knew also that what he was feeling was something that was sweeping across the world. He had been part of unleashing a new spirit, a new way of seeing the world and others.

Perhaps Atlantis would actually rise and work with humans again; perhaps the rising was just a wave of peace in people's hearts.

Only time would tell.

Right now he just wanted to laugh and clap his hands.

::: twenty-one :::
A Family Affair

permitte divis caetera
leave the rest to Heaven

Now was the time for speeches.

Back in the Great Hall, a great circle took shape, but this time there was a centre stage upon which Queen Fara was seated. Phantoam and the other dragones were outside the circle, on the fringe, but carefully positioned over an area of gold so any possible leaking fluid from their stomachs would not damage the floor of the hall itself.

The three musical elves Martin had met on his very first visit to Queen Fara's palace were joined now by a group of elfin children that played instruments Martin had neither seen nor heard before. They were mostly string instruments. The children were of all ages – there seemed to be no restriction or ruling, here, as with the cooking or the gathering of food. There was one troll, though, looking very uncomfortable (perhaps he was new) with a long trumpet-like wind instrument. It was the first time Martin had seen a troll play anything.

The band struck up and a sweet and melodious sound floated across the Great Hall and bounced off the walls, resonating inside everyone.

Morduainè stood next to Martin, his hand on his shoulder. He looked down at him and smiled: "Don't worry, we just want to thank you. And to give you a present. I think we also have a surprise for you."

"A surprise?"

"Yes, a surprise," said Jezze-B, having come from nowhere. "We want you to remember us," she said smiling, moving her eyebrows up and down – something Martin had noticed her doing since his last conversation with her.

Trollip was suddenly beside Martin also.

"Remember us, remember us. OOOooooee! Yes. I remember *your* face in the Dark Woods!" And he began to laugh, taking Martin's hand in a gesture of gratitude and respect, and pumping it up and down vigorously in his own version of a handshake. It left Martin almost exhausted, with Jezze-B laughing out aloud as she flitted this way and that with much excitement.

Martin looked at Trollip, his first friend in Tantalis, and well remembered his entrance that fateful night; his fear, and the excitement of realising he had a mission, a renewed strength and purpose. He smiled when he realised that it had taken this long and arduous journey to learn that the real key had been inside him all the time.

And it had all started with this one ugly-looking troll.

And a box.

A surprise?

He thought hard, but nothing logical came to mind.

What about his own tricorn?

A troll as a slave? – no! That was bad thinking, and he smiled shyly at Trollip who stood next to him. What about his own magic table to take back and keep his friends busy with fascinating pictures and images of Tantalis? – perhaps they would then believe him when he told them the tales of his adventure.

He shook his head. His own baby dragone!

That was it! He could just imagine Bleaney Davinporte's look when Martin took the dragone to class. He would teach it to breathe its fetid breath all over Bleaney's face and burn the yellow pimples on his nose!

Martin began to laugh out loud.

Once again the gentle spirit of the new Tantalis, this old Atlantis, rose and everyone laughed with him. And then he realised that they could all see what he was thinking. Oh, no! He would just *have* to remember not to think anything bad when there was any attention focussed on him in public!

Queen Fara beckoned for him to come forward. She stood now, her long creamy garment flowing in unison with her white hair down to her feet, bare and almost invisible.

Martin found himself, as with so much in Tantalis, transfixed – he could hardly keep his eyes off her and what she was wearing – the patterns in her garment seemed to change shape and form, and they behaved like a kaleidoscope – changing each time he looked at them.

Had Kyla paid special attention to her again?

Martin had found out her secret from one of the faeries on their march. Queen Fara's skin glowed magnificently and although it looked somewhat otherworldly, Martin fell to the spell of her beauty and found that tears welled up in both his eyes. The assembly grew silent, obviously viewing in the console Martin's very thoughts; trolls and elves bowed their heads, some with tears in their own eyes. But what was it that they were seeing, or feeling? thought Martin.

Martin knew then that he could be in love, and even though he felt embarrassed, especially considering this was someone probably old enough to be his mother, he still felt the birth of something wonderful. Something that would rest within him until it was ready to reveal itself fully.

Queen Fara stood up and placed her arm around him. She addressed the assembly.

"It is not easy being any kind of human. There are temptations and many difficulties that also accompany much pain – this is often difficult for most of us to understand. We experience different emotions, but the malicious and dark human-pain is something we have left far behind.

Martin has had his own share of pain; but more than most he was called to do something no human has done before.

He was called upon to walk when he thought he could not. He was asked to go places other humans might have told him simply do not exist. He was asked to do things so many felt were impossible. We honour and love you for this, Martin."

Martin shifted slightly from one foot to another; he was clearly a little embarrassed, and tried really hard not to entertain any barefaced thoughts, fearing they might appear to everyone present. But when he looked across at the console, and the column of light and images rose from it upwards towards the ceiling of the Great Hall, he could see himself, with a horde of Tantalians from all sectors of their society walking up the mountain, picking flowers and drinking at streams. It was an image he wanted to enter, feeling its powerful pull on him. Queen Fara interrupted his thoughts and continued:

"We might have stayed, happy and mildly content in Tantalis, enjoying her fruits and gifts, but we always knew the time would come to share the Power of Now – the very spirit of our lost Atlantis again with the human world. And you, Martin, made that possible."

She smiled at him and then beckoned to someone behind him.

"Ish-chaer, please come forward."

Queen Fara waited for him to climb onto the stage, and looked out at everyone gathered around her:

"Here before you, the first brave turned-Inkwa – I often wonder whether I might have had the courage to do what my honoured friend and confidant has done – alone, abandoned yet beckoned by both the light and darkness. Without guidance or assistance; with the spirit of Tantalis calling him back, yet with every fibre in his being telling him to stay. No one has done this before, or since without the opening of the Box. We honour you, we thank you. Perhaps it is even true that without your turning, we might never have had the courage or the opportunity to open it at all."

A great cheer went up from everyone in the Great Hall, rising, sweeping across and around the circle itself. Phantoam and some dragones cocked their heads backwards and spat huge flames up towards the colossal ceiling above, and clouding the columns that rose up with the flames themselves.

And the lonely troll, now a little more brave, blew his

trumpet-like instrument with such frenzy that he seemed to levitate.

Queen Fara handed Ish-chaer a small box – inside was a chain and pendant. When he opened the box and placed it around his neck, Martin could see its magic instantly. In the many shades of light as it turned like a mobile, an Inkwa appeared and then disappeared to show a clear image of Ish-chaer himself. It was neither a hologram, nor an image simply captured in a tube of light or glass – it was both and so much more; something truly astonishing.

Martin couldn't keep his eyes from it.

Queen Fara then turned to face Martin again.

"Martin, we have something for you, made by the trolls and then finished by Jezze-B herself – it took her a long time to make this as magical as she did."

Jezze-B squeaked with delight, right behind Martin.

"When you return home and wear it, now and then someone will come up to you and stare at it. You will then know that they also know, and that the world of humans is gaining ground, and people are turning and more are able to see what you can see."

She took out his own pendant from another blue box.

It was a beautiful key – exquisitely designed and masterfully carved in gold, looking just like the key Martin had carried and relied on so many times, but somewhat smaller.

Queen Fara handed it to him, carefully holding the chain between her fingers. The key dangled at the end of the chain, turning round and round, spinning so swiftly that Martin was afraid to come anywhere near it; he held out his hand, but then hesitated. Suddenly they key itself changed shape and form.

There before Martin's eyes was Trollip, and then, with another twist, Queen Fara and then suddenly Jezze-B; around and around it turned, spinning in the thick buttery light of the Great Hall itself, as though propelled by some magic.

It was something similar to the pendant given to Ish-chaer, but instead of being a block or tube of light itself, the key seemed to be the starting point of so many images – especially people who turned back into the key itself each time Martin seemed to blink; indeed each time he doubted that it was actually happening.

He sensed there was a great deal of magic present here, and something deep down told him, too, that more than just magic there was a power that would keep him, sustain him. Martin shook his head. Perhaps even take him further on another adventure.

And when it stopped turning altogether and came to rest,

a perfect image of his father came to life. Martin held his breath as his father smiled and waved at him from the end of the chain.

Martin waved back, tears welling up in his eyes. Perhaps he would not be able to bury him fully after all. He looked at Ish-chaer who was still next to him for some sign, some recognisable image or expression that would remind him of his father, but there was none. He simply looked down at Martin and smiled, his own special beautiful smile.

Everyone began to sing again, and the music flared up to fill the hall from one side to the other.

Then Morduainè came forward to congratulate Martin, and when he had done so he raised his hand, turning it as Martin had seen Queen Fara do in her first greeting. Everyone around him did the same.

Martin put the key around his neck.

"Was this the surprise?" Martin asked Ish-chaer, his voice faltering a little.

Ish-chaer raised his large eyebrows. "I don't think so. You will have to look somewhat further for that."

He pointed with his face and chin beyond them, to where the dragones were resting on their stomachs. At first Martin could make out two people – they seemed to be standing next to Phantoam, talking to him. Then they began to walk towards him.

They looked neither like trolls nor elves; they were taller and looked even less like faeries. Martin was convinced, suddenly, that they were not at all from Tantalis. But where – another world as yet undiscovered? Was this in itself the surprise: new creatures?

But then the light from the opening in the ceiling above fell on them like a spot-light; they were nearer now.

And there was no mistaking who they were.

Both Martin's mother and Dominika were running towards him; his mother with her hands up against her face, and Dominika with the golden locket Phantoam had give her, now bobbing up and down against her body as she ran. They were smiling also.

Martin was running too until finally he fell into their arms; all three of them laughing and crying at the same time.

And then suddenly the laughter and cheering of everyone in the Great Hall drowned the music that flooded the hall itself – the music that would remain with the three of them for a long time.

And as Martin felt the arms of his mother, and those of his best friend around him, something told him it was time to go home so that others could hear it too.